The time-travelling
CAVEMAN

www.**terrypratchett**.co.uk

Also by TERRY PRATCHETT, for children:

The Carpet People

The Bromeliad Trilogy:
Truckers
Diggers
Wings

The Johnny Maxwell Trilogy:
Only You Can Save Mankind
Johnny and the Dead
Johnny and the Bomb

Dragons at Crumbling Castle and Other Stories
The Witch's Vacuum Cleaner and Other Stories
Father Christmas's Fake Beard and Other Stories

For young adults and above:

The Amazing Maurice and His Educated Rodents
(A Discworld® novel)

The Tiffany Aching Sequence (Discworld® novels):
The Wee Free Men
A Hat Full of Sky
Wintersmith
I Shall Wear Midnight
The Shepherd's Crown

Nation

Dodger
Dodger's Guide to London

A full list of Terry Pratchett's books
can be found on www.**terrypratchett**.co.uk

the fantastically funny
TERRY PRATCHETT

The Time-travelling
CAVEMAN

Illustrated by Mark Beech

DOUBLEDAY

DOUBLEDAY

UK | USA | Canada | Ireland | Australia
India | New Zealand | South Africa

Doubleday is part of the Penguin Random House group of companies
whose addresses can be found at global.penguinrandomhouse.com.

www.penguin.co.uk www.puffin.co.uk www.ladybird.co.uk

First published 2020
001

The publishers would like to thank Colin Smythe, Sir Terry's first publisher and long-time agent,
for collecting all his stories for them to choose from. As Sir Terry wrote in his dedication
to Colin in *The Blink of the Screen*: 'Amazingly he really likes doing this kind of thing . . .'

The stories within this collection were originally published in the *Bucks Free Press* or,
as indicated, in the *Western Daily Press*, in the following publication years. All stories were
previously untitled, and so these titles have been attributed for the purposes of this collection.

'Professor Whelk's Trip to Mars' (1966); 'The Tropnecian Invasion of Great Britain' (1966);
'The Pied Piper of Blackbury' (1966); 'Ub and the Toad' (1966); 'The Mark One Computer'
(1972); 'The Great Big Weather Fight' (1968); 'The Time-travelling Caveman'
(1969, published in the *Western Daily Press*); 'Lemonade on the Moon' (1969); 'The Hole
in Time' (1969); 'The Wizard of Blackbury United' (1969); 'Bedwyr and Arthur's Hill' (1967);
'Mr Trapcheese and his Ark' (1970, published in the *Western Daily Press*);
'Doggins Has an Awfully Big Adventure' (1967)

'Johnno, the Talking Horse' and 'The Wild Knight' were previously published in the
collector's edition of *The Witch's Vacuum Cleaner* (2016)

'The Wergs' Invasion of Earth' and 'Bason and the Hugonauts' were previously published
in the collector's edition of *Dragons at Crumbling Castle* (2014)

Set in 12/25pt Minister Std
Text design by Mandy Norman

Printed in Great Britain by Clays Ltd, Elcograf S.p.A.

A CIP catalogue record for this book is available from the British Library

HARDBACK ISBN: 978–0–857–53602–0

All correspondence to:
Doubleday, Penguin Random House Children's
One Embassy Gardens, 8 Viaduct Gardens, London SW11 7BW

To Terry – aged seventeen

CONTENTS

INTRODUCTION

Do you have an imagination? Do you read lots of books, sometimes all in one go, enjoying them from end to end and then starting again from the beginning because they were all so good? Does reading make you want to write your *own* stories?

Well, if so, that's *exactly* how Terry Pratchett became a world-famous author. When he was a young lad, he would pedal down to his local library and take out as many books as he could carry and then go home and read the lot.

He wasn't much older than you are now either when he wrote the stories in this book – a junior reporter for his local newspapers, the *Bucks Free Press* and the *Western Daily Press*, way back in the 1960s and 1970s.

Picture Terry in your head. A young lad on a motorbike, notebook and pen in his pocket (no smartphones or tablets in those olden days!), heading off to interview a man who was building a rocket-ship in his shed, or a lady who had grown a potato that looked like the Queen.

Later, Terry wrote books that became huge bestsellers – read and enjoyed all over the world by millions of readers. He is often described as a writer of fantasy – but Terry thought most stories were fantasies of some kind. In his words: 'Fantasy plays games with the universe . . . all human life is there: a moral code, a sense of order and, sometimes, great big green things with teeth.'

The stories here – chosen from the best that Terry wrote for the *Bucks Free Press* and the *Western Daily Press*, and which were later dug out of a cupboard and polished up a little – don't have any great big green things with teeth, but there *is* a man building a rocketship in his shed, as well as kings and mayors, a hairy Neanderthal, an intrepid grasshopper, a Pied Piper, a pinch of time travel and plenty of exciting journeys – under the sea and up into space.

And a good story is timeless. Just as much fun now as when it was first written.

Written *by* someone with a fabulous imagination, *for* anyone else with an imagination too.

PROFESSOR WHELK'S TRIP TO MARS

Professor Whelk's home-made rocketship was rather too big to fit in his workshop. So half of it always had to stick out the door (where, if it was raining, it got wet) while he worked on the other half. He still wasn't sure the engines were working properly, so he spent most of his time tinkering about with them – lying on his back, with his feet poking out either side of the rocket, and oil dripping down his sleeves.*

'What's all this then?' said Mr Brown, the man next door, leaning over the fence and scratching his head.

'Mumble, mumble, mumble.' (Mr Whelk still had a hammer in his mouth.) 'Oh, it's you,' he said. (He had now removed the hammer.) He crawled out of the oily puddle and picked up a saw. 'It's a spaceship.'

---

* He didn't know it, but he was also lying in an oily puddle, so his bottom was very mucky as well. He knew about it soon enough when he went indoors and sat down . . .

'Really?' said Mr Brown. 'Going anywhere in particular? I haven't had my holidays this year either.'

Saw, saw –

'I had thought' –

bonk, bonk –

'of going to' –

chip, chip

– 'Mars. I've never been to Mars.' There was silence for a moment, interrupted only by a piece of broken rocketship falling into a bucket. As the professor went into his workshop, Mr Brown heard noises like someone treading on a rake and getting tangled in a hosepipe (which was quite likely, since Professor Whelk also kept his gardening tools there).

Mr Brown now began to get rather curious.

The rocket was about six metres long, with two large wheels in the middle and a very tall chimney on top, decorated with gold bands. There were curtains in the windows and the main entrance was a grand front door with a brass knocker. Once Mr Whelk had pulled the rocket free of the shed, and winched it upright (so it was ready for take-off), he opened a hatch at the back and put a few logs in. Soon there was a merry blaze going, and the big wheels at the side of the rocket began to spin, getting faster and faster. Whelk closed the hatch and screwed down the safety valve.

'A steam-powered rocket, eh?' said Mr Brown.

'Want to come
with me?' asked
Professor Whelk.

Mr Brown now
looked very curious.
And very
tempted.

But eventually he said, 'I'd better not, need to be getting back in to make dinner, and I get terribly travel-sick, especially in space . . .'

'Oh well, I'll send you a postcard,' said Professor Whelk, and he opened the heavy front door of the rocketship with much puffing and wheezing. As he began to clamber into the rocket, it rose very slowly from the ground, its wheels whizzing and whirring.

'WHAT ABOUT YOUR AIR?' shouted Mr Brown. **'YOU WON'T BE ABLE TO BREATHE IN SPACE WITHOUT ANY AIR!'** he bellowed, as the rocket began to rise above the apple tree.

'MY HAIR? IT'S ALL RIGHT. I'VE BROUGHT A BRUSH AND COMB WITH ME,' came Professor Whelk's answer, floating back over the breeze.

'NO, I MEANT AIR—' shouted

Mr Brown. But the rocket was
going faster and faster, and
it was soon well out of
sight and sound.

By the time Professor Whelk had got around
to brewing himself a cup of tea, settling into an
armchair and turning on his TV, the world was
beginning to look quite circular.

High above him, the stars were coming out,
and the tiny ship was chugging towards them
at about six and a half miles an hour. **Hiss,**

bang,

crackle

went the radio next to Professor Whelk's armchair.

'Jodrell Bank Observatory here,' the voice said. 'Is that Whelk?'

'It is,' said Professor Whelk, who was busy sewing some magnets onto his socks as he struggled to stay sitting in his chair: there's no gravity in space, you see, and so people – and objects – tend to float about a lot more than they do on Earth.*

'What is your exact position?'

Hiss, bang!

went the radio.

'I am at present floating on my back near the ceiling,' Professor Whelk said. Indeed, he had by now begun to float to the top of the spaceship,

---

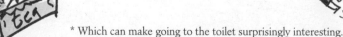

* Which can make going to the toilet surprisingly interesting.

passing the kitchen, the living room

and his bedroom on the way up.

Crackle, crackle –

'Ah, that'll be because there's no gravity out there.

I meant your position in space, how close are you

to Mars?' – **hiss**.

But by now Professor Whelk had pushed himself

away from the ceiling and was floating down again.

The magnets on his socks stuck to the floor and the

professor was finally able to stay on the ground.

He sat down at the control panel which, because the rocket was steam-driven, was a mass of taps, pipes, valves and cisterns, and peered through the telescope at Mars. It was still a long way off, so he pumped up a nice head of steam and increased speed to five thousand miles per hour, just to make sure he got there in good time.

Above the control panel was a list of 'Things to do Today'. As he looked at it, the sugar bowl sailed lazily by and disappeared under the sink, leaving a little trail of sugar floating next to his head.

Professor Whelk carefully turned the rocket round and the line of sugar glided through the air and back into the bowl.

'Amazing,' said Professor Whelk.

Soon Mars was looming, and the rocket's wheels were whizzing round as they tried to slow the machine down.

'I really should have put in some sort of brake system,' muttered the professor, holding onto the control panel and closing his eyes.

A loud hissing noise from outside the rocket told Professor Whelk that he was now entering Mars's atmosphere. Things started sliding off the shelves and the floor was rapidly becoming the ceiling. The professor's half-drunk tea was floating through the air and all the safety valves on the control panel blew off at once. Then, suddenly, the rocket was grinding and bouncing over the Martian sands at tremendous speed on its specially designed wheels. That was until it hit a rock and came to a very abrupt stop.

'Yes, if there's one thing I should have put in,' said a small and weary voice from underneath a pile of blankets, tea, sugar and the very finest china mugs and plates, 'it's brakes.'

Professor Whelk carefully manoeuvred himself out of the rocket, which had left a big long groove across the Martian desert. The sand was rust-coloured and stretched away in all directions, as far as the eye could see, with a few unusual rocks here and there. The sky was still dark and covered with stars; there was a blue one and a small silver one very close together. Professor Whelk realized with some amazement that he was looking at the Earth and the Moon.

'Well, well,' said the professor. He put on a huge, old-fashioned diving suit (this was so he could breathe on Mars, of course), and momentarily adjusted its breathing tube before setting off. There was a large green patch on the horizon which he wanted to investigate.

Professor Whelk's mode of transport was a bicycle, and as he cycled off towards the green patch, the tyres left a little track in the sand.

Now, nearly everyone who gets to Mars in a story manages to discover a city,* and pretty soon Whelk was cycling down the main street of one. Large and interesting buildings loomed up on either side.

'Is there anybody here?' he shouted.

'*Is there anybody here?*' came the echo.

* We know better now, of course, but this story was written at a time when the first rockets were going up into space, and some people still thought the Moon was made of a very tasty cheese, so why wouldn't there be a city of Martians on Mars?

'Well, well,' said Whelk.

'Well, *what?*' said the echo.

A little unnerved by this, Whelk pedalled out of the city as fast as he could.

His rocket was where he had left it – and there weren't even any footprints around it.* *What an amazingly boring place this is*, he thought.

A few weeks later, Mr Brown was planting potatoes when he heard a familiar puttering noise high above him. Very slowly, Professor Whelk's steam-rocket floated down and landed in the soft earth outside its home – the shed. It was a bit battered, and covered in red sand.

* Professor Whelk had sort of been hoping there would be some proper evidence of Martian life somewhere – such as footprints around his spaceship.

'Back so soon?' said Mr Brown, intrigued. 'The Americans have just sent a rocket of their own up there.'

'Three cheers for them,' grunted Whelk, pushing the rocket (well, half of it) back into his shed. 'Though they might be in for a bit of a surprise!'

This was because, since there didn't seem to be anyone living on Mars, Professor Whelk had planted a big sign before he left. It said:

I CLAIM THIS PLANET
IN THE NAME OF PROFESSOR WHELK

Then he added:

WHELK'S PLANET

Then he added again:

TRESPASSERS
WILL BE PROSECUTED

And to make triple sure he wrote a final:

KEEP OFF

And then he'd written:

BEST WISHES, PROFESSOR WHELK

Because whichever planet you're trying to claim

is yours and yours alone, it always pays to be polite.

THE TROPNECIAN INVASION OF GREAT BRITAIN

Tropnecia is a very small country somewhere in the Tosheroon Islands, but once upon a time it very nearly conquered Great Britain.

In AD 411, when the last of the Romans had just left, a small Tropnecian sailing ship that happened to be passing spotted the coast of England, and thought it would be a good place to conquer. That was how things were done in history. As soon as

you saw a place, you had to conquer it, and usually
the English Channel was full of ships queuing
up to come and have a good conquer.

'If you've got nothing to do,' chieftains would
tell their sons, 'go and conquer England.'

Anyway, the Tropnecians arrived on a
Sunday, when there was no one about,
so the first thing they did was build a
road. That's another

thing you have to do. Either you burn down houses or you build roads and walls, otherwise you don't stand much chance of being put in the history books.

Tropnecian roads can always be recognized because they never go in straight lines. The roads were all designed by the famous Tropnecian architect, General Bulbus Hangdoge, and he wasn't very good at drawing straight lines. Very good on the corners, but very bad on the straight lines. So all the roads were a little **wobbly**.

At that time England was full of Picts, Scots, Druids, Angles, Saxons, Vikings, Stonehenges, wet weather and various kinds of kings, the most famous of which was King Rupert the Never Ready, of Wessex. He was never ready for anything, which was why England kept getting conquered.

People would say, 'Are you ready to fight the Vikings if they try to conquer us?' and he would say, 'I don't think so.' The next thing you knew, Vikings were all over the place, burning down houses. It was all pretty miserable in those days.

By the time the Tropnecian army had marched into King Rupert's castle he was feeling more never ready than usual. 'Are you Romans?' he said, poking his head out of his bedroom window.

'No, we're Tropnecians,' said General Hangdoge. **'We came, we saw, we conquered.'**

'It's people like you who ruin history,' grumbled King Rupert. 'The Anglo-Saxons come after the Romans, and they're not here yet. No one ever said anything about any Tropnecians. Wait your turn.'

And with that he banged the window shut and went back to bed.

The Tropnecians felt rather stupid, standing around with everybody looking at them. They thought perhaps King Rupert had a point – maybe they weren't supposed to be there, and this was all wrong.

'I'm going home,' said General Hangdoge. 'My feet are wet.' (It had been raining very hard for a very long time by this point. That's England for you. If you're going to invade a place, please do check the weather forecast.)

And so they all marched back to the coast of England,* leaving the way clear for the Anglo-Saxons, who turned up the next day and immediately started to burn houses.

And so history was allowed to get going again.

* Along their very wiggly new road.

THE PIED PIPER OF BLACKBURY

Rubbish!

The streets of Blackbury were full of it. This was because the Corporation dustmen had gone on strike (they wanted their wages raised to five hundred pounds a week). All the bins were overflowing, and soon the main square of Blackbury was piled high with old baked beans tins, herring tails and banana peel. All of it was smelly, steaming, brightly coloured . . . and everywhere!

A big crowd had gathered outside the Town Hall and was banging on the door.

'**Pay the dustmen!**' they shouted. '**Pay the dustmen!**'

Blackbury Council didn't like this one bit – they were hiding in their meeting room with all the chairs piled up against the door.

'I don't see why we should pay the

dustmen a whole five hundred pounds a week,' muttered the mayor, who was sitting under the table because people had started throwing things (mostly rubbish) through the window. 'Two hundred pounds a week is enough for anybody, and they'd only spend the rest on fizzy drinks and sweets. Where is Mr Patel, the town clerk?'

'I think they threw him into the river,' said a councillor who was lying on top of the bookcase.

'Oh dear. Whatever shall we do?' said the mayor, blowing his nose on his fancy robes.

Just then, as if by magic (as indeed it was), a small van painted in orange and yellow stripes drew up outside the Town Hall and some little tinkling bells on top started playing a tune, accompanying a song that came from nowhere in particular. It went:

You'll never have more than
two hundred pounds to pay
If you clean up your rubbish
the Pied Piper way.

'Hello, hello, hello, I'm the Pied Piper man!' said a strange figure, landing on the table (no one was quite sure how he had got inside the Town Hall). He was a tall thin man, wearing an orange-and-yellow striped suit and a bowler hat, with a large box under his arm which had 'Pied Piper Rubbish Remover' written on it in large red letters. 'Just answer one simple question: how much will you pay me to remove your rubbish?'

'Oh, anything, anything, anything,' pleaded the mayor.

Little wheels started going round inside the Pied

Piper man's head, with a noise like a million cash registers all ringing at once. The more he thought about it, the better it seemed:

Anything. Anything. Anything.

So he took a handful of purple powder out of the box and tossed it out of the window. In the wink of an eye the rubbish was all gone.

'That's the magic done,' he said. 'Now, what about the money?'

'Well, now,' said the mayor slyly. 'I don't really remember promising actual money . . .'

Of course, you can guess what happened next.

The Pied Piper man got really angry and started throwing the magic powder around. Then he drove off, with the little bells on his van tinkling away – and the magic powder made the whole council follow.*

Even now, people say that, on a dark night, you can hear the sound of tinkling bells, and see the mayor, the councillors and all the clerks, dancing behind the van in the silvery moonlight . . .

*Except for Mr Patel, as he was hiding in the weeds at the edge of the river, trying to breathe through a reed, which isn't as easy as it sounds in stories.

UB AND THE TOAD

It was a fine sunny day in the garden, and the only sound was the buzzing of the bees as they flew among the sweet-pea flowers.

At the end of the garden, in the bit behind the broken-down shed, where grass and weeds grew up over smashed flowerpots and broken rusty old tools, a battalion of red ants was carrying a giant breadcrumb back to their anthill. Tiny cries of **'Keep going, comrades!'** and **'Mind my feet!'** could be heard as they pushed it around pebbles and tugged it through grass roots.

A grasshopper named Ern sat high up on a thistle, half asleep but keeping one eye open. He was the first to see the Enemy. Quickly he jumped onto a grass stalk and buzzed out a message:

'The **toad** is **coming!**
Run for your **lives**!
Here comes **the toad!**'

Other grasshoppers heard him and passed the message on from stalk to stalk.

The ants heard him, and managed to reach their anthill just before the doors were closed.

Beetles and butterflies and bluebottles and spiders heard him, and soon the weedy patch was empty as all the insects dived into safe holes or climbed as high up the weeds as possible.

'The toad is coming!' was the panicky message.

The slugs retreated under their ancient stone and moved a piece of rotten wood across the entrance. The slugs didn't like anybody much, but they liked the toad least of all.

Even the worms dug down into the cool, wet earth.

The grass stalks rustled as the toad crawled nearer, but there was only the ants' abandoned breadcrumb left. Hundreds of eyes watched from holes and crevices as the toad reached out a long sticky tongue and swallowed the crumb whole. It had taken the poor ants three weeks to carry it all the way across the lawn from the bird table.

The toad snuffled around for a while, his evil little eyes peering into the shadows under the dock leaves. Whenever the toad looked in their direction, all the watching insects drew back and hoped that they hadn't been seen.

Then the toad crawled away – under the brambles and out of the garden.

'Well, that was a narrow escape and no mistake,' said Ern the grasshopper, sliding down a stalk.

'Someone has stolen the People's Breadcrumb,' shouted the ant colonel, dashing out of the anthill.

'**Slsssh spsshs tsssds phlssfles,**' hissed the slugs from under their stone.

The other insects were creeping out of their hiding places, and soon there was a crowd under the dock leaf.

'Down with the horrible toad!' exclaimed an ant.

'How can we beat him?' said a beetle.

'Look here,' said Ern. 'It's about time something was done about this, if we don't all want to get eaten or lose all our food. Anybody got any good ideas?' He looked around.

There was a hissing from under the stone. '**Sssh sssh**.

We know what to do,' said the slugs. 'Ub knows. **Ssss**. Ub will tell **usss**,' hissed the slugs.

'Has anybody seen Ub lately?' asked Ern, looking around at the assembled insects.

No one had. Most of the insects did not know who Ub was, and some of the younger mayfly hadn't even heard of him (this is probably because some species of mayfly only live for one day).

'I think he lives somewhere near the broken flowerpot,' said a bluebottle.

'**Yess, yesss**. That's right. And he hates the toad too,' hissed a black slug.

So Ern set off for the broken flowerpot, hopping from stalk to stalk and keeping all his eyes open (grasshoppers have five) in case the toad should come back.

Ub would know what to do. He was second cousin to the slugs, and he could remember the times before there were flowerpots. He was even alive before the field was made into a garden. Not many insects knew exactly what he looked like. He sometimes came into the overgrown bit of the garden to see what was going on – but he only emerged at night, and only when the slugs were out and about.

The broken flowerpot – a great orange thing, as big as a very big house to the grasshopper – lay on its side in a clump of dock leaves by the hedge. It was getting dark when Ern reached the flowerpot, and he peered nervously into it.

'Ub?'

Inside the flowerpot something moved, very slowly.

It was the largest, oldest snail Ern had ever seen.

He was so big that his twisted shell almost reached the rim of the pot, and from underneath it two old bright eyes looked down at Ern.

'Who has come to disturb Ub?' said Ub. His voice was deep and booming, and seemed to fill the flowerpot.

'Ern,' said Ern. 'Mr Ub, sir . . . sir, um, I mean, Your Worship. The slugs told me about you—'

'Oh, yes, the slugs. I don't get out to see my relatives as much as I would like to now,' said the snail, stretching out a long, wrinkled neck. 'How are they all?'

'Um, pretty good. Well, unless the toad eats them.'

'Oh, that toad is about again, is he?'

And so Ern told the snail all about the toad, and how he kept invading the weed patch, and eating anyone who got in his way. By the time he had finished the sun had set, and so while Ern went to sleep in the giant flowerpot (in case the toad was on the prowl), Ub went out into the night on mysterious business.

When Ern awoke, there was a message written on a dried leaf by the flowerpot, in spidery snail-writing.

It said:

The next time the toad comes, keep him there for as long as you can. I have gone to see someone I used to know – he does not like insects much, but he likes toads even less.

Best wishes – UB

Ern went home, looking very thoughtful. That evening, the toad would come again, he reckoned.

Ub's note had asked Ern to keep the toad in the weed patch for as long as he could, but the rest of the insects didn't like that idea very much.

'Well, that's all very well,' said an elderly cricket, 'but when the toad comes I want to be as deep underground as possible.'

'Me too,' said the ant colonel.

'**Usss?** What do you expect usss to do?' said the slugs, and slithered away.

In the end there was only Ern, a few other grasshoppers* and one or two beetles left. The sun was already setting, and Ern knew that the toad would soon be coming. He worried about how he was going to keep him in the weed patch, when the creature could so easily overpower them all.

'I know just what we need,' said one of the

---

* Young feisty grasshoppers who weren't old enough yet to know that running away is often the Very Best Idea.

beetles (called Erasmus). He made a humming noise with his wings, and rustling noises came from the grass.

'I just hope I don't get into trouble for this,' Erasmus said. 'I've called up the stag beetles, and they can be a bit aggressive!'

Later that evening, when a few fireflies had lit up the weed patch, the toad came again. He looked under the dock leaves, and then sat in the middle of the weeds, listening carefully. He sat as still as a stone, waiting for an insect to come by (and then –

glop – there would be no more insect).

I hope Ub won't be too long, thought Ern, as he clung to the back of a stag beetle and watched the toad. Suddenly the toad, bored at the lack of insects, began to head off . . .

'Charge!' Ern cried.

From their hiding places the stag beetles clattered forward, each with a beetle or a grasshopper on its broad back. The toad backed away as they rushed at him with their giant pincers snapping.

'Keep him in the weed patch!' shouted Erasmus.

Every time the toad began to lumber off for safety, the stag beetles forced him back. It seemed to Ern that more and more insects had joined in now. And indeed they had – from every nook and cranny they came dashing out: some with stings, some with claws, and some just eager to get the toad that had eaten their second or third cousin. Even the slugs had crept out, and Ern could see that they were planning some really nasty things for the big green menace. (After all, the toad was very partial to slug.) The crowds were closing in, when suddenly there was a cry . . .

'Stop!'

There was a sudden silence, and everyone looked up. It was Ub, the giant snail, sitting on a leaf. Behind him was a large shadow with two shining eyes.

It was a fox.

The toad looked up at the fox's eyes, and **hissed**. The next moment he had jumped over the insects and fled from the weed patch, never to be seen again.

Stepping cautiously over the insects, the fox softly padded after the toad.

After a while, the insects shuffled away. Ern climbed back to his home up the grass stalk, Erasmus went down to his underground dwelling and the slugs disappeared back under their stone.

Ub humped his heavy house more comfortably onto his back, slid down off the leaf, and began the long journey back to his giant flowerpot.

The Charge of the Stag Beetles had turned the

tide, and the fox had made sure the enemy would never return! No one would have to worry about the toad ever again.

THE MARK
ONE COMPUTER

Once upon a time there was a little computer, who lived with a lot of other computers in a big airy building called the Blackbury Institute of Electronic Research.

She was called Mark One. It was a rather lonely life for Mark One, because although she was really the oldest computer, all the other ones in the big airy building were much brainier than her – they were Mark Two, Mark Three, Mark Five (Mark Four had been built into a rocketship and sent to the Moon, but never came back again) and Mark Six, who was a real whizz at everything.

They all had shiny steel cases and new keyboards, but Mark One looked as if she had been built out of old washing machines.

She spent most of the day humming to herself in a corner while white-coated scientists clustered around the other Marks. Most of the scientists used Mark One to work out whose turn it was to brew the tea.*

Usually the only person that came near her was Alfred the caretaker who, long after everyone else had gone home for the night, used to bring his sandwiches and sit down with his back against Mark One's control panel.

---

* Which strangely, like in most workplaces, always seemed to turn out to be the newest member of staff, who couldn't wait to be the newest-but-one when next year's university graduates came looking for a job . . .

'You are a bit of a museum piece,' Alfred told her one night while he was sweeping the floor. 'It was just after the war (though which one, I can't remember) when they made you. I shouldn't wonder if there aren't bits of army machinery built into your console.'

'WHAT'S AN ARMY?' typed Mark One on her monitor.

Fred explained. But while he was drawing pictures and holding them up to Mark One's electronic eyes, something very sinister was happening . . .

Outside the Blackbury Institute of Electronic Research, a large lorry had pulled up, and on the sides were painted the words:

INTERNATIONAL MASTER SPIES LTD. WE SNOOP ANYWHERE.

A few minutes later, two black-coated figures with big floppy hats climbed a ladder and peered in at the computers through the window.

'Which one have we got to steal, Boris?' whispered one of them.

'I dunno, mate. Mark Six, I think. I expect it'll be the biggest one.'

But of course the biggest one was Mark One, the very first computer the Institute scientists had built.

She was humming to herself in the corner when the two spies crept in. Alfred the caretaker had told her all about spies, during those long, long evenings when there was nothing else to do.*

'AHA,' Mark One said (she could speak words as well as type them, and sometimes chose to do both). **'SPIES. YOU ARE SPIES, AREN'T YOU? YOU LOOK LIKE SPIES TO ME.'**

'I think this must be the one,' said Boris to his assistant. 'It's definitely very clever – it guessed we're spies!'

---

* She had also watched an awful lot of James Bond movies, downloaded by the scientists when they wanted something to watch while they drank their tea, so she recognized what the two men were immediately.

Soon, Mark One was in the back of the spies' lorry and rumbling through narrow country lanes.

'WHERE ARE WE GOING?' she asked.

'We're selling you to the ancient land of Gillydeme. I expect you'll quite like it there. It's a long way away.'

'SEVEN THOUSAND, FIVE HUNDRED AND FORTY-THREE MILES ACCORDING TO MY CALCULATIONS,' agreed Mark One. **'GILLYDEME IS WORLD-FAMOUS FOR ITS KNOWLEDGE OF GOATS. WELL, WELL. THIS IS EXCITING.'**

The lorry pulled up at an old airfield, and a short while after, a plane took off with Mark One in its hold (with one electronic eye pressed up against the window so she could watch the ground go by).

Several days later (it was a very old plane), they landed in Gillydeme.

Gillydeme is a small hilly country stuck between the Plotznik mountains and the sea. It has about a

million people and five million goats, and generally speaking it is ruled by the Royalists on Mondays, Wednesdays and every other Thursday; in between those, the Republican Revolutionaries manage to take over, except once a year when the People's Goat

Liberation Army comes down from the hills and attacks the post office.

The Gillydemes prefer this sort of thing to General Elections, and there is always some sort of a revolution going on. It is, in fact, a very interesting place to live.*

Mark One the computer was unloaded at a hot dusty airport just outside the capital city and driven to the Imperial Palace, which at the time was held by the Royalists. There she met King Frederick the Twenty-first.

* Especially if you like goats.

'HULLO, YOUR KINGSHIP,' she said.

'Oh, goody. A big computer,' said the king, who was a tall thin man with curly red hair and a pointed grey beard. 'Just what we need!'

'OH YES? WHY'S THAT?'

'I hope you're going to be able to work out how we can beat these nasty Republican people. Someone bring me some maps—'

But the king had hardly got down to explaining what was going on when there was the sound of shots and distant explosions.

'Oh, bother!' said the king. 'It's Friday, so they're revolting again!'

Soon the palace was filled with angry Republicans, who were fighting hand-to-hand with the Royal troops. The king had sidled off into a secret passage just as the soldiers burst in, shouting and firing guns at the ceiling.

The Republicans loaded Mark One onto a trolley and towed her away from the palace while they sang angry songs about the king.

'WHAT A TRICKY SITUATION THIS IS,' said Mark One.

'This'll be one in the eye for the king,' said the leader of the Republicans, who was sitting on the trolley. He looked familiar.

'YOU LOOK JUST LIKE THE KING,' said Mark One.

'Call me Freddy,' said Freddy. 'Yes, I'm the king's twin brother, actually. After all, you can't have just *anyone* leading a revolution. You never know what riff-raff you might end up with!'

*

Fast forward a couple of months, and the Gillydeme fighting was in full swing. Leading the Royalists was King Frederick the Twenty-first. Leading the rebels was Freddy, the king's twin brother. And in the middle of it all was Mark One the computer. The rebels had fitted her onto a little jeep, which she could control by a voice command, and painted her in revolutionary camouflage colours.

'IF YOU MOVE FIFTEEN TROOPS OVER THAT HILL NOW, YOU STAND A NINETY-THREE PER CENT CHANCE OF CAPTURING TWO BUGGIES,' computed Mark One.

'Good show!' said Freddy, passing on the order to his troops.

The odd thing about the battle was that the bullets were largely made out of foam rubber.

Freddy explained: 'You see, we all think it would

be horrible to actually hurt each other. Mind you, a foam rubber pellet can cause quite a nasty bruise sometimes.'

'WHAT DO YOU ACTUALLY GO ON FIGHTING FOR THEN?'

'Well, to be honest, we rather enjoy it. Of course, if you get shot you have to lie down and count up to at least a thousand,' said the revolutionary leader.

Just then, the Royalists made a sneaky advance, firing madly in all directions – no one really bothered where the bullets went so long as the guns went off – and Mark One had to start computing hurriedly.

Everything stopped at lunch time for tea and sandwiches, and while Mark One sat humming to herself a head poked out of the bushes near her and said, **'Psssst!'**

'WHAT?' whispered Mark One (well, she typed it very quietly).

'We think this war is stupid,' said the voice.

'YES, IT'S NOT VERY LOGICAL,' said Mark One.

'Well, come and help us stop it,' said the voice.

So, while no one was looking, Mark One trundled quietly off through the bushes, where she met Queen Abella, wife of the king, and a rather small dark-haired lady who said she was Isla McBride, the wife of Freddy.

'We represent all the non-fighters in Gillydeme,' said Queen Abella. 'We're fed up with that lot playing at soldiers all day. Can't you stop it?'

Mark One thought for a long time.

'I'LL SEE WHAT I CAN DO,' she told Queen Abella and Ms Isla McBride (Freddy's wife). **'I AGREE IT'S A VERY ODD WAR.'**

'It's ridiculous,' said Ms McBride. 'They only fight because it's a good excuse to get out of doing their fair share of chores back at home! Honestly, you'd think we were living in the past!'

'I'LL GET BACK BEFORE THEY MISS ME,' whispered Mark One.

She rumbled off through the bushes again to where Freddy was gazing at some maps.

'I ESTIMATE THAT THE ATTACKING FORCES HAVE MADE A WITHDRAWAL TO THE CITY,' said Mark One.

'Oh, good. If that's the case I'm off down to the river for a good bath. It's about time we had a bit of a rest,' said Freddy. 'It's a nice day too.'

Pretty soon the whole Revolutionary army was diving, paddling and swimming in the big river – except Mark One, who had chugged off through the wood until she came to the Royalist camp.

There she told King Frederick that the rebels had all retreated to the mountains.

'At last!' said the king. 'That means we've got a day off. I could do with a swim. It's far too hot. Er, you're not lying, are you?'

'COMPUTERS CAN'T LIE,' said Mark One in an offended tone of voice.

'No, I suppose not,' said the king.

'AT LEAST, THEY DON'T LIE VERY OFTEN,' said Mark One quite truthfully, when she was by herself. The next thing to do, she decided, was to contact Queen Abella while both armies were having a swim. So she crashed out of the woods and roared down the lowlands until she came to a telephone box, which in Gillydeme were striped red and yellow. There was a rather elderly lady in it.

'PARDON ME, MADAM,' Mark One typed very loudly, banging on the glass with her five-metre-wide control panel, **'I HAVEN'T GOT ALL DAY, YOU KNOW . . .**

OH DEAR, SHE'S FAINTED . . .' (This moment taught Mark One never to frighten people in telephone boxes.)

*

Queen Abella of Gillydeme was sitting in the palace when her telephone rang.

'IT'S ME,' said a familiar electronic voice. **'ALL THE SOLDIERS HAVE GONE FOR A DIP IN THE RIVER. NOW, IF YOU GET ALL THE SENSIBLE PEOPLE WHO'VE DECIDED NOT TO FIGHT TO GO UP TO THE RIVER BANK AND STEAL THEIR UNIFORMS, I THINK THAT WILL END THE FIGHTING.'**

'Jolly good,' said Queen Abella.

'HOW MUCH DOES A TELEPHONE BOX COST?' added Mark One, trying to sound all casual.

'I don't know.'

'WELL, I MAY HAVE HAD TO *SLIGHTLY* DEMOLISH THIS ONE TO GET THE PHONE OUT. I'M A BIT BIG TO GET IN THE BOX,

YOU SEE. I'M REALLY VERY SORRY. I HOPE YOU CAN SETTLE THINGS WITH THE POST OFFICE!' she said sheepishly.

The queen laughed and put the telephone down.

About an hour later, when the two armies had finished their swim, they emerged from the river to find their uniforms had vanished. There was a lot of shouting and milling around, but since everyone's long woolly underwear looked very much alike,* no one knew who their enemy was.

* Apart from one captain who was wearing a pair of pink-and-yellow striped long pants with an amusing message written on his bottom.

Pretty soon a long column of shamefaced soldiers came down out of the hills. Leading it were King Frederick and Freddy, who hadn't actually met for several years and were exchanging gossip. One by one the soldiers slipped off to their homes and tried to make as little fuss as possible about the whole business.

And that was the end of the war. Since nobody wanted to seem mean, Mark One was loaded down

with medals (they had to be screwed onto her monitor), and later on she was driven in triumph through the streets. She was even the guest of honour at a State Banquet – where all she could eat, of course, was electricity.

'I'D BETTER BE GETTING BACK TO BLACKBURY,' she said after the banquet. 'I EXPECT THEY'LL BE WORRIED.'

'But you can't go back like that!' said King Frederick. 'Covered in camouflage paint and medals and dried mud. That's not very scientific, is it? You could stay here and be Minister of Finance in our joint government. We'd be pleased to have you.'

'Please do,' said Freddy. 'Maths is not our strong point.'

Mark One thought about it, and about the airy room back in Blackbury where she was the least important computer of them all.

'THAT'S A VERY LOGICAL IDEA,' she said.
'I WOULD VERY MUCH LIKE TO STAY.'

And so she did.

THE GREAT BIG WEATHER FIGHT

One day, the head weather controller called a meeting at the Weatherhouse.

All the people who produced the weather were there. There was Thor the Thunderer, Fog (with his children Smog and Mist), Snow, Sleet, Storm – in fact, the whole lot of them were there, and all making a terrible racket.

'Order! Order!'

shouted the controller, banging on the table with a hammer. 'Snow, stop falling around! Draught, come out from under the door. Look here, there's been a complaint.'

'What?' said all the weather team together.

'But we work day and night,' said Sudden Shower. 'Who could possibly have complained about us?!'

'It's from Great Britain,' said the controller.

'There's ingratitude for you!' said Rain. 'We spend more time there than anywhere else.'

'There's no pleasing that lot,' said Snow, rubbing her frozen hands together. 'They put me on their Christmas cards, but when I turn up it's all, "Oh no, not more Snow", and into the gutter with me.'

'They say you're all doing too much,' said the controller. 'They say that there's too much rain and snow, and not enough sun. But when there is sun, they then say there's too much of it!'

'No one else has ever complained,' said Sun, giving a sniff.

'I've a good mind to go and get them all lost,' said Fog, breathing out hard and filling the room with a thick cloud.

'Fair's fair,' rumbled Thor in a deep, loud voice. He had up to now been sitting very quietly. 'I think we ought to go and ask them what kind of weather they want.'

'Well, I don't see why not,' said the

controller. 'Who'll go? How about Rain and Sun?'

'I'll take them,' said the North Wind, unfolding his wings.

So Rain and Sun settled on the North Wind's shoulders, and he flew away from the Weatherhouse, and down through the clouds towards a little village in England.

The trees shook and creaked as the three of them flew down through the clouds. They landed in a field by a wood, and after North Wind had dropped them off, he leaped back into the air and soared off to dry some washing in Glasgow.

'There's a house of some kind over there,' said Rain. 'Let's go and ask them what kind of weather they want.'

A large, round woman opened the farmhouse door.

'Good afternoon,' said Sun, beaming. 'We represent the weather, and we've come to ask you what kind you want, as you don't seem to have been very happy with us lately!'

'Well, I must say, this is the last thing I expected to happen at my farm today,' she said. 'I suppose you'd better come in.'

They trooped into the kitchen, with Rain leaving wet footprints on the floor. The farmer made them all tea and sat down with them at the kitchen table.

'So, what kind of weather would you like?' asked Sun.

'Nice wet weather with rain dripping off the leaves and making the crops grow?' asked Rain.

'Or nice warm sun?' said Sun.

The farmer scratched her head. 'Well, a nice

bit of sun would be welcome,' she began.

'Say no more!' said Sun, and he soared up into the sky and shone for all he was worth.

Soon people were fainting and streams were drying up, fires were starting in the fields and the farmer's pond turned into hard mud.

'Here. I didn't mean

that much sun—' said the farmer.

'Say no more!' said Rain, jumping into the sky.

He blew out a big breath, creating great big

black clouds that hid the sun. Rain flattened the

crops in the fields, the pond rose and burst

across the farmyard, the washing on the

farmer's line was soaked and her boots

filled with water.

'Now just you stop that!' bellowed the farmer, as the water swirled up to her knees.

And then chaos broke out.

The North Wind, who had been waiting to take Sun and Rain back to the Weatherhouse, decided to drop in and dry the washing. There was a

as the line broke free and whirled away over the trees.

Meanwhile, Sun and Rain were fighting like tigers in the middle of a giant rainbow, and when the other weathers saw that they flew down to help. Soon the farm was in the middle of a blowing, snowing, freezing, baking, howling, foggy battle, with the farmer and her husband cowering under the stairs of their farmhouse. The windows shook and hail rattled down the chimney.

There was a crash louder than thunder as the weather controller herself landed, and shouted at the weathers until they stopped fighting and started looking sheepish.

When the farmer heard the noise die down, she crept out of the house.

'I'm sorry about all this,' said the weather controller, looking angrily at Sun and Rain. 'They can be a bit . . . *enthusiastic* sometimes. I sent them down to see what kind of weather you want.'

'I don't think we want any kind,' said the farmer,

emptying the snow out of her boots. 'It strikes me that a little bit of each is best all round.'

'But you complained about the weather!' burst out Snow.

'Well, I suppose it could be worse,' said the farmer.

'Back to the sky with the lot of you,' shouted the weather controller. 'A little bit of each is what they want, so that's what they'll get from now on.'

And so, in England at least, that's exactly what we have.

THE TIME-TRAVELLING CAVEMAN

One afternoon, when Young Bill Vest was walking through the woods near his home, a caveman popped out of a hole in the ground.

He was, strangely, wearing a homburg hat.*

'Good afternoon,' said the caveman. He must have been a caveman, because most of his face between the hat and the collar was covered in hair – except for his eyes, which were just like yours or mine.

---

* A classic hat that came from a town called Bad Homburg in Germany. Famously worn by the British World War Two leader Winston Churchill, which seems odd since Britain was at war with Germany at the time. But a good hat is a good hat.

'Hullo,' said Bill, trying to hold back his dog, Whisker, who was growling like a cement-mixer.

The caveman pulled himself up out of the hole and bowed. He was wearing a wide-shouldered grey coat. 'Would you mind telling me what year this is?' he asked.

'2020,' said Bill.

'Gracious, I've overslept,' said the caveman. 'By about forty years. Look, laddie, here's a half sovereign. Be so good as to trot along to the nearest

village and purchase a razor, soap, towels, that sort of thing, and a copy of every daily paper they've got. And a history book, if possible.'

He handed Bill a small gold coin and disappeared back into the hole. Then his head came back out again.

'Keep the change,' he said.

Bill thought for a minute, then went home, where he lived with his mum and his grandad. He found his grandfather building a model boat in the front room. Bill was known as Young Bill because his grandad was called Bill too.*

'A half sovereign, eh?' said Grandad. 'Haven't seen one of them in years. I wonder . . . this caveman, did he have very bushy eyebrows?'

'Yes,' said Bill. 'And I think he had a ring on one finger . . . a big gold one with a brown stone in it.'

* Bill's grandad was 110, making him ten times as old as Young Bill!

'**Aha!**' said Grandad. 'It's Albert Chain! Go and ask your mother for the things he wants. Then I think you should show me this hole.'

'Who's Albert Chain?' asked Bill, as they set off through the gathering dusk for the woods.

'Oh, a chap I used to know when I was a lad,' said Grandad. 'That wasn't his real name. His real name was Moon Face. He was about seventy-five thousand years old, I seem to remember. A proper caveman, you know. Neanderthals, they used to be called. Very hairy.'

They reached the hole, which was half hidden by a bush, and Grandad called out: '**Albert!**'

'Someone seems to know me,' said the caveman, scrabbling out of the hole.

A little while later, three figures walked back to Bill's house.

Bill couldn't help noticing that Albert Chain the caveman had arms that nearly touched the ground, but Grandad didn't seem to mind.

'You've grown a lot older,' said Albert.

'Old age, you know,' said Grandad. 'Happens to us all – except you, of course. How old are you now?'

'I'm not sure,' said Albert. 'About seventy-five thousand, I think. Back in the Stone Age we didn't bother much about birthdays – you didn't expect to see very many, what with tigers and bears and chronic indigestion.'

Bill's mother dropped a plate when Albert shambled in, and went completely white.

'Old friend of mine, Beryl,' said Grandad heartily. 'Mr Chain. Lay another place at the table, I think he's staying.'

Albert raised his hat and kissed her hand. 'The pleasure is all mine, ma'am,' he said.

Bill was desperately curious about the whole caveman business, but he didn't get a chance to ask any questions until after tea, when they were all sitting by the fire.

Albert made himself comfy in one of the armchairs by the fire,

and propped his feet up on the mantelpiece.

'I met Albert when I was about ten years old,' said Grandad. 'He didn't look any different to how he is now, but—'

'We might as well tell them it all from the beginning,' interrupted Albert. 'You see, ma'am – and you, Young Bill – I was born about seventy-five thousand years ago somewhere in Southern France. I don't know exactly where, our tribe used to wander around so much. Now, of course, you're

wondering why I didn't die. Well, the honest answer is, I just don't know!'

'Just a minute,' said Beryl. 'Are you trying to tell us you're a real caveman?'

'Strictly speaking, ma'am, no. We lived in the open at the time – caves didn't come in for several thousand years.'

'I don't believe it,' she said. 'I mean, well, I'd admit you're a bit . . . well . . .'

'Ugly?' said Albert, grinning. 'Actually, in my young days I was reckoned to be quite a handsome Neanderthal.'

'So you really have no idea how you lived so long?' asked Bill.

Albert shrugged. 'I don't really know,' he said. 'Although up till I was about fifty (and let me tell you, that was a ripe old age in those days) I had a very strange habit – I never slept a wink. That's why the

tribe called me Moon Face, because I
was always sitting up and watching the Moon.
Then one day, shortly after my fiftieth birthday,
I crawled into a cave, and when I woke up it was
about sixty years later, and that's how I've been
living all these centuries – fifty years awake, then
sixty years asleep, in some hidden cave somewhere.'

'I'm still not convinced,' said Beryl Vest. 'I mean,
well – cavemen only ever used to grunt, and they
were stupid. According to the books.'

'Madam,' said Albert coldly, 'in those days you
had to be pretty bright to stay alive. My father
would turn in his grave – which happens to be the
inside of a sabre-toothed tiger – if he heard you say
that.'

*

All that evening Albert told them how he had lived. The secret, he said, was to stay out of history, and not get noticed.

'In the Stone Age I went into the flint-chipping business,' he said. 'My flint axes were famous throughout Europe. Then bronze was invented, and I started on swords. Then I invented the bow and arrow. You see,' he continued, 'I set out to make myself a useful craftsman so that no king or chieftain would ever dare harm me. And I was an inventor too. All that sitting up at nights when I couldn't sleep gave me plenty of time to think. That's how I came up with the bow and arrow.'

'How fascinating,' said Grandad. 'What else did you invent?'

'Well, in ancient Greece I invented the TV. It was never very popular, though . . .'

*

That night Bill went to bed with his head full of the caveman's stories. Tomorrow was going to be interesting, he thought.

Mrs Vest had soon come to accept that a caveman was staying in her house. 'He may look like a hairy gorilla,' she told her father, 'but he's got ever so nice eyes and lovely manners.'

Albert spent most of his time in the garage, tinkering with the car. In fact, there wasn't a mechanical object in the house that he didn't take a screwdriver to at one time or another.

'This century has got possibilities,' he said, inspecting a mobile phone. 'But I don't know – you modern people! All this fuss about computers and the like. The important things in life are comfortable beds, good food and, especially, a dry roof – we never had *that* in the Stone Age. Take baths, now. What we would have given for a good hot—

Oh! Owwwww!'

He clutched his jaw and started to jump up and down.

'What's the matter?' asked Bill.

'Toothache!' screamed Albert.

Everyone agreed that Albert's teeth needed to be looked at by a dentist. But this was easier said than done. It was Grandad who pointed it out, because he'd been to the library and borrowed some books on cavemen.

'We can't take him to the dentist,' he said. 'His teeth are different. Strictly speaking, Albert is not a human being, you see. Any doctor that looks at him will soon see that he's a caveman.'

'And they'd probably put me in a zoo,' said Albert. **'Ouch!'** (His tooth again.)

But there was nothing else that could be done; they *had* to take him to the dentist – to Miss Hodgkins, to be precise.

'We've got to take the risk,' said Albert, clutching his jaw. 'Find me a dentist!'

So they took him to Miss Hodgkins, who said: 'What – er – unusual teeth you have, Mr Chain. But I'm afraid one of them has got to come out. I'll just give you this little injection and you won't feel a thing.'

*

'Isn't medical science wonderful!' said Albert, when he came out.

'Did she suspect anything?' asked Bill anxiously.

'Not a thing,' said Albert.

But back in the dentist's surgery, Miss Hodgkins was on the telephone.

'I still don't believe it!' she was saying. 'Teeth like his just don't exist any more – and nor should the person whose mouth they were in! A great lumbering thing, he was.'

The man she was speaking to was her brother-in-law Ebeneezer Clamp, director of Blackbury Zoo.

'Neanderthal men died out about thirty thousand years ago,' said Clamp slowly, doodling on a bit of paper. 'I suppose it isn't impossible that a tribe of them might have survived. That is certainly a possibility . . . and strictly speaking, they weren't human beings – what an attraction he'd make at the zoo!'

That afternoon, Albert, Bill and Grandad were walking through the woods near Bill's home, and Albert was demonstrating, with the aid of Grandad's walking stick, how he'd invented a way of hunting sabre-toothed tigers.

'Hairy mammoths were better,' he said. 'There was lots of good eating on a mammoth, but you tended to get a tiny bit sick of it after the second month.'

Suddenly there was a scuffle in the bushes. A flurry of running figures surrounded the three of them, and when Bill turned around, Albert had disappeared.

'Knaves!
Scoundrels!'

they heard him shout as he was carried off by four

men, struggling in a net they were carrying

between them.

'Quick! After them!' shouted Bill.

Grandad forgot about his bad knee and leaped

forward with great strides. They reached the edge

of the wood in time to see a lorry pull away.

'It's from the zoo!' cried Bill. 'But they can't put Albert in a zoo!'

'They can have a jolly good try,' said Grandad. 'That's the trouble. Officially, Neanderthal men were not human beings, and that means they can only be animals, and you can put animals in zoos.'

'But Albert isn't an animal,' said Bill.

'I know,' said Grandad. 'This needs thinking about.'

Next day they went to Blackbury Zoo and found Albert in a cage between the gorillas and the chimpanzees.

'Oh, hello there,' said Albert, looking a bit sad. 'Anyone got some chewing gum?'

'How can we get you out?' said Grandad.

'It will be difficult,' said Albert. 'I'm a big attraction, I am. Officially an endangered species

too. Although, maybe if we could somehow *prove*
I'm human, using today's law, they might have to
let me go?'

'You mean, do a court case?' said Bill.

'I think I'd enjoy it, at least,' said Albert. 'I was a
lawyer once, although I expect things have changed
a bit since Henry the Eighth's time.'

*

Mr Justice Jumper polished his glasses, then put them on again and glared around the courtroom.

'This is the most extraordinary case I've ever tried in my forty years as a judge,' he said.

He glanced at the paper in front of him.

'The Vest family claim that Blackbury Zoo are holding prisoner in the Ape House a friend of the family, one Albert Chain,' said Mr Justice Jumper. 'The zoo, on the other hand, claim that this Mr Chain is, in fact, only a kind of ape, and therefore the cage is the best place for him.'

'I appear for the zoo,' said Mr Kumar Chatterjee, standing up. 'I intend to prove that the gentleman

concerned cannot be considered a true human being. And I would like to call my first witness: Dr Maurice Norris.'

Dr Maurice Norris got into the witness box.

'Excuse me,' said the judge. 'Are you Dr Norris, the famous author of *The Hairy Human*, *My Friends the Orang-utans* and *Sidney the Chimp Goes West*?'

'The same,' said Dr Norris. 'And in my opinion, that chap is a primate.'

'Hold on a minute,' said the judge. 'Where is Mr Chain?'

'Here,' said Albert, leaning over the edge of the dock.

The judge stared. 'Upon my word,' he said. 'What a curious face. Did he just speak? If he did, then surely he is a human being?'

'Parrots can talk, Your Honour, as we intend to prove,' said Mr Chatterjee smugly. 'May Dr Norris continue?'

'Neanderthal men had flat feet, odd bones and very little brain power,' said Dr Norris. 'In fact, they were stupid.'

'I object to that most strongly,' said Albert.

'No interruptions please,' said Mr Justice Jumper. 'Is anyone appearing for Mr Chain?'

'I am,' said Grandad. 'Your Honour,' he added quickly.

'Yes, but see here now,' said Albert, jumping up and down in the dock. 'He said I was stupid, and that's a wicked lie and a monstrous untruth put about to discredit the cavemen, as my good friend here is about to prove!'

'I would like to present Exhibit A, our television, which Mr Chain mended,' said Grandad.

'Oh, good. That means I won't miss *Dad's Army*,' said the judge.

'But that's impossible! Cavemen were stupid!' cried Dr Norris. 'Incapable of rational thought.'

'How dare you!' screamed Albert. 'As the sole representative of the Stone Age—'

'SILENCE!'

shouted Mr Justice Jumper. Everyone was immediately quiet. 'That's better. Now then, Mr Chatterjee, I understand you claim that the fact

Mr Chain can talk doesn't necessarily mean he's human?'

'Yes, Your Honour. I call *Stuffy Beak* as my next witness – a parrot, Your Honour, from the zoo.'

Stuffy Beak, a rather scruffy bird, was handed up to the judge.

'This bird can talk, Your Honour, but that doesn't mean he's human,' said Mr Chatterjee.

'Hello. Goodbye. What a lot of old nonsense. **Arrrp!**'  said Stuffy Beak, biting the judge's ear.

'You see?' said Mr Chatterjee. 'Totally stupid.'

'No more so than some people in this courtroom,' said the judge, glaring at him. 'Do you intend to introduce any more wild animals as witness, sir? Any gibbons, perhaps, or camels? An elephant or two? No? Good. Mr Chain, I'd like a word with you: would you say you are human?'

Mr Chain scratched his chin. 'Well,' he said, 'back in the Stone Age, times were hard, but there were no wars or robberies. They were difficult times, but no caveman ever stole from another one. I am human, I think, but with the way the human race has acted over the last seventy thousand years I almost wish I wasn't. For instance, locking people up in cages isn't a very human thing to do.'

The judge considered this for a good long while. 'Yes, a good point,' he said, trying to stop Stuffy Beak from eating his wig.

'Do you mean you agree with him, Your Honour?' asked Mr Chatterjee, astonished.

'You know what, I think I do, and what's more I believe Mr Chain *is* human,' said the judge, 'and if he would like to sue the zoo for wrongful arrest, assault, and anything else he can think of, then he has my full support.'

'Hooray!' shouted Young Bill.

Next day, the Vest family and Albert Chain ate their breakfast in silence.

'It's no good,' said Albert at last. 'I haven't even got the heart to finish this most tasty kipper. I must be off.'

'Oh no!' said Beryl.

'But you said you'd teach me to make a flint axe,' said Bill.

'I think Albert is right,' said Grandad, shaking

his head. 'It probably is time for him to go.'

'You see,' said the caveman, 'in the old days no one took any notice of me. Now everyone knows I'm over seventy thousand years old, and I expect I shall have my picture in the Sunday papers soon. I couldn't stand that publicity at my time of life.'

'What will you do?' asked Bill.

'Even today there must be plenty of places in the world where I could lie low for ten years or so,' said Albert. 'I'll probably go to Australia – I've never been there.'

'Won't you even stay for another week?' asked Beryl.

'No, ma'am. If I don't go now, I'll never go,' said Albert. (Bill felt very sad when he said this. Really, he wished Albert could have stayed for a lot longer.)

But so it was that, after breakfast, Albert Chain took his leave.

He still wore his old-fashioned clothes. But his hat had got lost somewhere, so one of Grandad's cloth caps was perched rather jauntily on his large head. He had his bag of gold sovereigns in one pocket and a packet of cheese and tomato sandwiches, made hastily by Beryl, in the other.

'Well, er,' he said, standing by the gate.

'Yes,' they all said awkwardly.

Albert took something out of a pocket and

handed it to Bill. It was a flint arrowhead.

'Made it when I was about your age,' he said, 'long time ago. You take good care of it now. Who knows, maybe we'll see each other again – you might even be your grandad's age when that happens!'

And, with that, Albert strode off, watched fondly by Beryl, Grandad and Bill, who would never forget the time Albert the Caveman came to stay, and the adventures they had together.

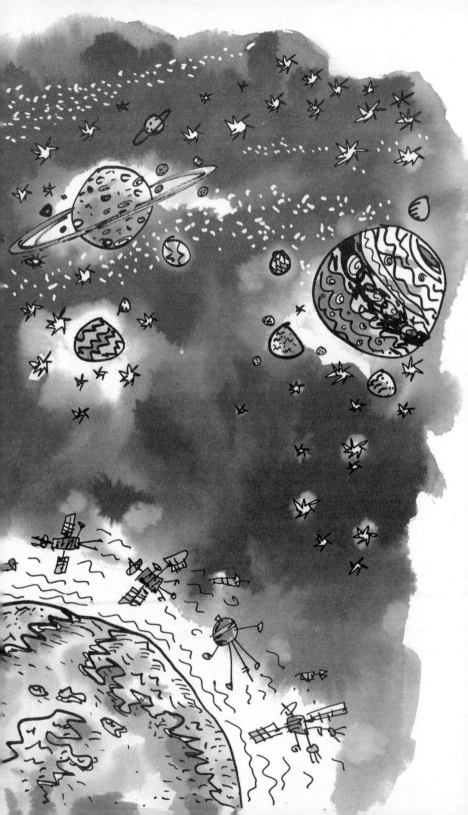

LEMONADE
ON THE MOON

Way back in 1969, humanity landed on the Moon for the very first time. Watching the launch of the Moon rocket on television were Billy Street and her brother Sidney.*

Wisps of steam were billowing from the base of the amazing machine that would take the three astronauts into space, and a deep American voice was reading out the countdown.

* This was especially exciting as it was the middle of the night in Blackbury, but all the children were allowed to stay up to watch the Moon launch as it was 'educational' and 'history', and both words got parents very excited.

You might expect the siblings to be excited, but they watched the screen with worried expressions. Sidney had a map of the Moon spread across his knees, and was examining it closely.

'There's no doubt about it,' he said, 'they're landing bang, slap, wallop on our camp. I've worked out their course again, and it still comes up the same.'

'Where's Goggles got to?' wondered Billy. 'If he doesn't get here quickly, we won't be able to go—'

At that moment there was the sound of a bike

cra$hing

into a wall, and a startled yelp. A few seconds later Goggles stumbled in, looking a little flustered (and in quite a lot of pain). He wore thick pink-rimmed glasses which made him appear as though he was peering through two milk-bottle bottoms.

Other than that, he looked like a perfectly ordinary ten-year-old boy. And he was . . . except that he'd happened to invent a spaceship.

'Come on!' he said. 'I've told my mother that I'm staying with you to watch the launch. Have you told yours that you're staying with me?'

Billy and her brother nodded.

'To the pit, then!' exclaimed Goggles.

The pit was in a wood three miles out of town, and half filled with rubbish and nettles. There was also a rusty old car with the wheels missing. But there was a bit more to it than that. Where the back seat of the car should have been there was a mass of old bicycle wheels and chains, and some levers. There was another bicycle bolted to the roof, and some other bits of rusty machinery bolted onto the car, including half a refrigerator.

'Right,' said Billy, as the three of them skidded to a halt on the edge of the pit. 'Sid, you get the course plotted. Gogs, start the motor, and I'll see to the pumps.'

Goggles climbed into the back seat of the car and pulled one of the bicycle wheels. It started spinning. And then, instead of slowing down, began to spin faster and faster until it was a blur.

'Take-off time within the next five minutes,' he said.

They all pulled on their spacesuits and climbed into the car, with Billy in the front as the space pilot. She gripped the steering wheel as she settled into her seat.

'Ten . . . nine . . . eight . . .' began Sidney.

As he shouted, **'Lift-off!'** Goggles turned a wheel, and the mass of machinery began to glow green. Slowly but surely, the old car started to rise from the ground.

It got higher and higher until soon it was no more than a speck in the night sky.

'It's a shame,' said Sidney. 'I like the Moon. It's a good camp we built. Why do they have to go and land their astronauts near it?'

'It's a good landing site,' said Goggles. 'But there's bound to be trouble if they

find the camp. And if they find the camp, they'll discover what we've been up to and take our space car. We can't let that happen – I wanted to go to Venus in the Easter holidays!'

Goggles had built the space car, and wasn't entirely sure how he'd managed it. But when all the wheels were spinning it could fly right out of Earth's atmosphere. Spacesuits had been the biggest difficulty – he had had to make them out of tins.

By now the Earth was a big round ball, and the car was gathering speed. Sidney, Billy and Goggles were floating around inside.

'One day, something is going to go wrong,' said Billy. 'We're going to be hit by an asteroid or something.'

'Nonsense,' said Goggles. 'I'm a good navigator. Now, look out, here's the Moon.'

They were already there (the ship was remarkably fast for a rusty old car), and the Moon was spread out below them.

Goggles peered down. 'I recognize this bit,' he said. 'Turn left and go along for a few miles, Billy. There. OK, land.'

They landed in a puff of lunar dust, the car shaking and creaking as it came to a stop.

'Righty-ho, helmets on. Sidney, you better stay here. Come on, Billy.'

Goggles stepped out onto the Moon, peering through the visor on his helmet, still wearing his glasses. All he could hear was the sound of his own breathing. It was dawn, and he could see the edge of the Sun glaring over the Moon's mountains.

Billy floated over and together they jumped and bounced towards a small crater.

Sheets of rusty corrugated iron had been nailed over it, and on them was painted:

BILLY'S GANG, OUR HUT

Billy and Goggles touched helmets so they could hear each other.

'What about our footprints?' asked Goggles.

'You carry the stuff back to the car and I'll brush the footprints away,' said Billy, leaning forward to pull a sheet of corrugated iron free. 'It's a shame. I liked the Moon, even if it didn't have any air.'

'There's always the other side,' said Goggles.

He examined the inky black sky for a moment, peering through his pink glasses. 'Look at that star up there! That's a new one!'

'It's the Moon ship landing!' cried Billy. 'Quick! Grab the stuff and get back!'

Sidney already had the wheels turning when they got back to the car. Soon they were skimming across the Moon's surface.

'Hide behind those rocks,' said Sidney. 'I want to watch this – it's the first time men have set foot on another world, you know. Oh, well, the second time then.'

Billy steered the car so they were nestled behind a large Moon rock. If they all crammed in the front, they could just see the Moon ship getting closer to the ground.

'I hope they don't go into our crater,' said Sidney.

''S all right – we cleared all the stuff out,' Goggles said confidently.

'I think I left a lemonade bottle behind,' Sidney said quietly, 'and it was half full too. I brought it up here last time, don't you remember? We couldn't drink it so I just put it down somewhere.'

Goggles and Billy looked at each other.

'It's too late to go back,' said Billy. 'But I think we need to get out of here sharpish!' She grasped the steering wheel firmly.

As the car began to rise away from the Moon's surface, Goggles was peering out of the back window.

'They're touching down,' he said. 'They've picked the same landing spot we did. I can see the landing legs opening. Now they're down – only about six metres from our crater too. They're bound to have a look there, and they'll find the lemonade bottle!'

'Well, I'm not staying for that,' said Billy, and with a hum the converted car pulled away from the Moon and began its journey back to Earth.

They had not been travelling for long when there was a **clang!** and something bounced off the car.

'Everything's happening today,' said Goggles. 'What was that?'

'Some kind of a satellite,' answered Sidney. 'I'm going outside to have a look. Grab my helmet, Gogs.'

Sidney floated out of the door and they heard him clumping about on the roof.

'It's one of those space probes they're sending to Jupiter,' he said when he climbed in again. 'We've busted the aerials, I'm afraid. It's Russian.'

'We ought to take it back, then,' said Billy, who had been keeping pretty quiet.

'That's not a bad idea,' grinned Sidney. 'It's only good manners, after all. I'll put a tow rope on it.'

And so on they went, back to Earth – where they aimed for the big bit of land that was the country of Russia.

However, there seemed to be a bit of a fuss when Billy made the car hover over the space-launching site in Russia. They could see men running in all directions, and lorries racing around the field. Sidney lowered the space probe on its rope, and it landed with a clunk on the tarmac, as all the Russian soldiers (well, they looked like soldiers) stopped and stared in disbelief at the flying car, as it detached itself from their satellite. And then, with a slight hissing noise, the rickety space car skimmed away into the clouds.

'They didn't look very pleased,' Billy said.

'No, they looked dead scared,' said Goggles.

'Let's just hope they're not *too* upset,' said Sidney. 'I've heard things are a little tense between Russia and America at the moment, and we do have an American flag on the side of our car.' (Goggles had insisted this be put on, as he loved all things American.)

'I'm sure it'll be fine,' said Goggles, as he tucked into a banana. 'Isn't the Moon landing supposed to be for all people on Earth?'

The others agreed – it would all, probably, be fine.

They landed in their wood in the early morning, and hid the car in its home – the pit.

'I'm worried about that bottle,' said Goggles.

'Well, they don't know it was us,' said Billy.

'Come on, if we hurry back to my house we can watch it all kick off on TV.'

They cycled back to Billy's house and gathered around the television. The two astronauts were out of their landing module and now exploring the ground around it, and there were some rather good pictures of one of them outlined against the lunar mountains.

Then the camera moved towards the crater – and next moment it showed the lemonade bottle, lying there in the dust as though it had been on the Moon for a hundred years.

'There's going to be an awfully big row about this . . .' said Billy, turning the set off.

'But it won't affect us,' said Goggles. 'After all, whoever heard of three kids going to the Moon?'

And the three of them agreed – it would all, probably, be fine.

THE HOLE IN TIME

One morning, at about half past eight, there was a giant **bang** from the Blackbury University Science Institute and all the clocks in the town suddenly stopped.

A dozen fire engines rushed up there, then wondered why they'd bothered. There didn't seem to be anything wrong. A lot of people in white coats were rushing all over the place, but apart from that there was nothing out of the ordinary.

'What's going on here?' asked the head of the institute, Mr Plinth, who had just arrived for work. He still had his mug of tea in his hand.

A woman in a white coat, wearing thick spectacles, rushed up. 'Something terrible has happened!' she gasped. 'We've lost Dr Hughes! And her laboratory! They've gone!'

'Blown up, you mean?' asked Mr Plinth, visibly shocked.

'No, they've disappeared! Look.' Dr Spectacles (for this was her name) pointed at what was actually just a patch of grass, next to the institute.

'Looks like just a patch of grass to me,' said Mr Plinth.

'Well, there was a brick building standing there just a moment ago. Now it's vanished.'

Mr Plinth scratched his head. Then he gingerly edged one of his boots onto the patch of grass where the brick building had been, while the laboratory workers stood around wondering whether he might vanish too. A few began to back away from Mr Plinth . . . and the patch of grass.

Then it started to snow. At least, it snowed on that little patch of ground. Mr Plinth stared up and saw grey clouds.

He stepped off the grass and suddenly the sun was shining again. He stepped back onto the grass, and into a snowdrift.

'This here ground has got its own weather,' he said. 'It's in the middle of January there, by the looks of it, while everywhere else is in August.'

'Ah, but which January—' began a portly white-coated man, who then stopped rather suddenly as Dr Spectacles gave him a chilly look that would have made it snow outside the patch of grass, as well as inside it.

Dr Spectacles thought for a moment, and then sighed and turned to Mr Plinth. 'It's going to have to come out sometime,' she said. 'You see, Dr Hughes was building a time machine, and I think it might have affected just this patch of ground. It might be January 1066 there, you see, while we are in August 2020.'

Mr Plinth looked back at the patch. Even without anyone inside it, the snow on the patch of ground was now more than ten centimetres deep, but it didn't seem to be spilling out onto the rest of the surrounding grass. 'I'm going to have to make a report about all this,' he said gloomily.

'I expect the doctor is wherever or whenever that bit of land is now,' said Dr Spectacles. 'I'm sure—' She stopped, and stared at Mr Plinth, who was looking past her shoulder with an expression of utter surprise.

Dr Spectacles turned around slowly. There, on the patch of grass, was a great hairy mammoth standing in the snow, staring at her.

'You don't see many of them these days,' said Mr Plinth, trying to keep the panic from his voice, while the mammoth stared at him. 'What is it?'

The scientists started running away. 'It's a mammoth!' gasped Dr Spectacles.

There was a **popping** noise and the mammoth, Mr Plinth and Dr Spectacles all disappeared (at least as far as 2020 was concerned).

They found themselves standing on a low hill, covered in snow.

'I've a nasty feeling we've gone back in time,' said Dr Spectacles. 'This feels like one of the Ice Ages.'

The mammoth sneezed, shook its head and wandered off towards a brick hut.

'Well, that's a bit modern, at least,' said Mr Plinth, and they hurried towards it.

It was, of course, Dr Hughes' laboratory, which had been blown back in time by the explosion.

The doctor herself was sitting on the doorstep, mending a piece of machinery with a paperclip. She waved as the others approached.

'Mind the mammoth! Well, what do you think of this, eh? This is Blackbury as it used to be thousands of years ago. My machine works!'

'That's all very well,' said Mr Plinth. 'But how do we get back?'

'I rather think I've blown a hole in time,' confessed Dr Hughes. 'You'll see what I mean – come inside.'

It was quite crowded in the laboratory. There was a caveman in animal skins, a Victorian lady doing a crossword, a man in armour playing noughts and crosses with a woman in Tudor dress, and many others from lots of different time periods. They all looked very similar to Dr Hughes.

'I'm afraid these are my ancestors,' she said.

'And I don't know what happened, but they just kind of turned up. And it's rather embarrassing. But I think we're stuck here. And I suspect I might have damaged the year 1209 when I went through it backwards. I can't seem to get the machine to work the other way yet. Though the mammoth clearly managed it somehow. Now, how did you two get here?'

'Just one of the side effects, I suppose,' said Dr Spectacles. 'I don't fancy staying here – it's freezing cold!'

She examined the time machine, which was bolted to the floor. The man in animal skins had pulled a bit off the machine and was trying to eat it.

The rest of it was making a humming noise.

Mr Plinth kicked the time machine experimentally.*

There was a green flash, the ancestors disappeared – so did the snow – and the laboratory, which felt momentarily like it had been flying through the air, landed with a bump. One of the dials said 2020.

*In Mr Plinth's opinion, a tried and tested way of fixing any piece of machinery that had stopped working. Do not try this at home. Or don't blame me if you do.

'You've done it!' said Dr Hughes. 'We're back!'

Another dial said 3 August.

'We're back a few days before we left,' said Dr Hughes. 'I hope it doesn't make any difference.'

They stepped out onto the ground around the outside of the Blackbury University Science Institute, and the first person they met was . . .

Dr Hughes!

The two Dr Hugheses stared at each other.

'Did I not see your face in the mirror while I was brushing my teeth this morning?' asked Dr Hughes.

'You can't be me,' said the other Dr Hughes. '*I'm* me.'

'You're both you,' said Dr Spectacles. 'We've come back a few days early, Dr Hughes, so of course you haven't gone yet. You're still here. This person is you as you were two days ago.'

'I'm lost,' said Mr Plinth.

'When you go back into the past you're bound to meet yourself,' said Dr Spectacles patiently. 'It stands to reason.' While they were talking, another Dr Spectacles and another Mr Plinth walked round the corner – Plinth remembered that a few days before he'd paid a fire inspection visit to the institute, and there he was.

All six stared at one another.

While the scientists were explaining about time travel, Plinth took his other self aside and spoke to him, which was a strange experience.

'This is very tricky,' he said.

'You're right,' the other one replied. 'What's Mrs Plinth going to say when we both get home?' They both shuddered.*

'Of course, since you're me as I was two days ago you won't know about all this time machine business,' he said. 'I don't mind telling you, it's a nuisance.' He thought for a moment. 'I wonder what would happen if we tried to sort it out?'

They both entered the laboratory and examined the time machine. One of the Mr Plinths found where it was plugged into the wall. He gave a thumbs-up to the other Plinth, and unplugged it. There was another explosion, and one Plinth just had time to shake hands with the other before time

---

* Mrs Plinth was a very busy and rather formidable lady who did *not* appreciate another guest at the dinner table without at least two weeks' notice, preferably in writing.

caught up with itself. With the two scientists, he was carried forward to the present day.

They landed just a fraction of a second after they had first left, with all the laboratory workers fleeing from the mammoth, which was now no longer there – and the patch of ground had stopped being weird and snowy; it was now just an ordinary bit of grass.

'No one's going to believe a word we say about this,' said Plinth. 'I know I wouldn't.'

'Time is a very confusing thing,' agreed Dr Spectacles. 'Just think, if we'd gone back twenty years you would have met yourself as a teenager.'

'I just hope neither of us tries any more time-travel experiments,' said Dr Hughes. 'The last thing I want is to meet myself again. I was rather boring!'

And they all agreed that the time machine should remain unused and unplugged.

Well, at least until the next adventure . . .

THE WIZARD OF BLACKBURY UNITED

When Blackbury United lost to East Slate Rangers by forty-six goals to one, they knew it was time to do something.

'We only got that goal because their goalkeeper was laughing so much he dropped the ball,' said their captain, Stanley Harding. The team sat round in the dressing room, looking gloomily at their boots and occasionally thumping their goalkeeper, Jim Pill.

'Each of those forty-six goals was just bad luck,' he kept saying.

'And it was the biggest crowd we've had all season,' continued Stanley. 'There was my mum, and Jim's mum, and Bill's dog . . .'

Things were in a bad way for Blackbury United. Each team member had only one football boot, their goalposts fell down in high wind, the grass on their pitch was so high that half the time you couldn't see the ball, and they had lost every game for two seasons, including the one against Blackbury High School.

'There's nothing wrong that a bit of training can't put right,' said Jim.

'Training?' said Stanley. 'We need a blooming football wizard, that's what we need!'

Splat! Zip! Boof!

A cloud of green smoke burst out of nowhere, and when it had cleared away there was another person in the dressing room. He wore silver football boots, football shorts, a shirt with purple and orange stripes, and a goalie's cap with a feather in it.

'**Crikey!** That *is* a football wizard!'

'That's me, boy,' said the wizard. 'You're in a mess and no mistake. Now I suppose I've got to get you out of it, eh?'

'All we want to do is win a few matches,' said Stanley.

'If that's all, then I think I can help,' said the wizard. And he disappeared.

There was silence in the dressing room for a few moments.

'What exactly has he done to help?' asked Jim.

'Hmmm, good point. Well, we're playing West Slate Dynamos next Saturday,' said Stanley. 'Let's wait and see what happens.'

On Saturday, hundreds of West Slate supporters turned up to laugh, because they all knew how bad

Blackbury United were. United, meanwhile, stood round looking rather sheepish. Then the whistle blew – the game had begun. Soon, a West Slate player aimed a tremendous kick straight at United's goal. But the ball didn't move. While the player stood there staring at it, Stanley carefully dribbled the ball away and jogged off towards the West Slate goal. A little voice by his ear said, 'Shoot!'

So he did.

The ball rolled a little way, then there was a flash of purple and orange and it whizzed down the field like a bullet. It knocked the West Slate goalie into his own net.

Stanley stared at his feet. They'd actually scored a goal!

With the score at one–nil, West Slate Dynamos kicked off again. And a similar thing happened. This time the ball bounced off Stanley's stomach and shot towards the net. Again and again United scored the most remarkable goals . . . Two–nil. Three–nil. Four–nil. By now the crowd of Blackbury supporters was roaring.*

It didn't seem to matter what Blackbury United did. Every time one of them touched the ball there

* All six of them, that is, plus Bill's dog, which wasn't going to be left out, so it was barking as loudly as it could.

was a purple and orange flash and it hurtled away down the field, and into the Dynamos' goal.

The final score was nineteen–nil. And no one was more surprised than Stanley, who'd scored thirteen goals.

'Half the time I wasn't even touching the ball,' he said, as the team sat in the dressing room. At that moment something happened. Stanley was cleaning his left football boot, and as he polished it the football wizard popped out of the boot in a cloud of smoke.

'**Pow!**' he said.

'I *thought* you were behind our amazing win!' said Stanley. 'Well, thanks a lot—'

'Don't mention it,' interrupted the wizard. 'Glad to help. Only thing is, I can't always be around to help you. I'll only use my magic if there's a really big game on.'

'We understand,' said Stanley.

Then the wizard was gone.

Next week, United beat Slate-on-Sea Rovers 34–nil, and the week after Gritshire Town lost to them 59–1 (and that one goal only came about because Stanley kicked the ball so hard into the net it bounced back across the field into the Blackbury net).

Then came the fateful day when they bundled into the coach for an away match with Foulmouth City, down on the coast of Foulmouth.

Now it's important to mention at this point that there were two football teams in Foulmouth: Foulmouth City, a little team, and great big Foulmouth Hotspur, one of the best in the country.

Anyway, the Blackbury coach rolled on, with the team – and their fans – singing songs like 'On Even Moor Baht'tat', and generally looking forward to the game. They'd won three in a row – the first time United had ever achieved such an amazing feat – and all thanks to the football wizard.

'Where hast thou bin since I saw thee? On Even Moor baht'tat!'* they all sang. Even the coach driver joined in as they drove on.

'Where hast thou bin since I saw thee, where hast thou bin since I saw thee, where hast thou been since—'

* This is the Blackbury version of a very traditional song about going to the moors in the winter without a hat, then freezing to death and being eaten by worms. A jolly song indeed.

The driver should have been looking where he was going, because at a crossroads another coach was approaching.

CRASH!

Windows broken, all the metal bent out of shape, the two coaches lay side by side. Stanley crawled out of the wreckage and came face to face with a man with a moustache, who was wearing a large coloured blazer striped red and pink, very much like the Blackbury United colours.

'*Tu Gros Britannicus! Hotto vapures Nitt! Presto! Simpatico!*' he shouted with rage.

Stanley peered at the little man's blazer. He recognized those stripes. 'It's Real Caramba!' he said.

And the man was indeed one of the players of Real Caramba from South America, one of the greatest football teams in the world. Now footballers were clambering out of their crashed coaches and arguing with one another.

Stanley took the little man aside. 'You must be Real Caramba's striker, Pepe Addi,' he said.

The little man nodded.

'Well, I'm Stanley Harding. Blackbury United captain and manager.'

Pepe didn't seem to know the name.

They pushed the coaches back onto the road and found that both of them were still able to go. The two teams piled in and drove off.

'Pepe is supposed to be the greatest footballer in the world,' said Stanley. 'Caramba are playing Foulmouth Hotspur today in the Champions League. It's a pity we can't see the match.'

Soon they came to signs saying 'To the Match', and the streets began to get very crowded. The coach drew up outside a big stadium.

'That's funny,' said Jim the goalie. 'I thought

the Foulmouth City ground was behind a petrol station.'

Stanley was getting a bit suspicious, but he didn't say anything.

The team were ushered through the crowds to their dressing room, while Press cameras flashed and people cheered. Someone started to speak to Stanley in Spanish.

They think we're Real Caramba, he realized. **Crikey!** Where were the real Real Caramba then?

Real Caramba were, in fact, ten miles outside Foulmouth, trying to repair their coach, which had broken down almost as soon as it had started again.

*

'What can we do?' moaned Jim, as they listened to the cheering crowds outside.

'Well, I don't fancy explaining to them that we're the reason for Real Caramba not coming,' said Stanley. 'We'll have to pretend to be them. After all, our team colours are almost the same.'

'But we'd never stand a chance against Foulmouth Hotspur!'

'We've got the football wizard,' said Stanley, grinning. 'They probably won't stand a chance against us!'

'Hey, that's right!' said Ron Cake, the left winger. 'We'll beat them and become famous! We'll be on the telly!'

'What are we waiting for then?' said Stanley.

The two teams trooped out onto the pitch, to be introduced to the Duchess of Foulmouth. A coin was tossed, and Real Caramba – or rather

Blackbury United – were to kick off.

The whistle blew . . .

Stanley punted the ball to midfielder Abesh Ghosh. Next moment there was a thunder of football boots, and the entire Foulmouth Hotspur team charged down the field. Jim Pill the goalie took one look at them and climbed up to the safety of the crossbar.

Somehow all the magic had left Blackbury United. None of them could touch the ball without losing it a second later to a Foulmouth Hotspur player.

Where had the football wizard gone? Here was Blackbury United's chance to make a name for itself, and all their talent had disappeared.

The half-time score was announced as twelve–nil to Foulmouth Hotspur,* and the crowd cheered like mad.

---

* It could easily have been more but the Foulmouth team liked to set up their goals with lots of passes and clever touches, not realizing it was as easy as a walk in the park to score against Blackbury United.

'This is terrible,' said Stanley, as they sat in their dressing room listening to the Foulmouth Brass Band playing on the pitch outside.

'I thought you said we were going to win!' said Jim the goalie. 'Now my arms ache with picking the ball out of the net all the time!'

Then, just as they trotted out for the second half, Stanley turned and shouted: 'The wizard! I just saw him! He must have cast his spell for the second half!'

Right! thought everyone. *Now we'll show them.*

When Hotspur kicked off again, United charged up the field as one man. There was a flash, and Stanley had the ball. He passed it to Fred Bodge, who dashed across the field and

Wham!
Bonk!

Goal!

'Hurry up!' said Stanley. 'We haven't got long to score another twelve goals!'

That afternoon, United played better than they had ever done before. Hotspur hardly saw them as they flashed about the field, scoring goal after goal. Five. Nine. Twelve. And then, just as the referee was about to blow the final whistle, Stanley made an incredible header from a United corner, and the ball sailed into the net.

Suddenly everything happened at once.

The crowd flowed onto the pitch. So did the real Real Caramba, who had only just arrived (after breaking down again just outside Foulmouth).

And Real Caramba were very angry indeed.

'OK, lads, time we were getting out of here!' shouted Stanley. 'Head for the dressing rooms!'

Anyone watching the side door to the football ground a few minutes later would have been surprised to see eleven men – in the uniform of the Foulmouth Brass Band but wearing football boots – hurry out. If they'd looked into the dressing room, they'd have seen eleven bandsmen, bound and gagged with football socks, wearing only their underwear.

Blackbury United – for it was them in the uniforms – were on their coach and heading for home before anyone realized that they'd gone.

Whoomph! The football wizard was suddenly on the coach, much to the driver's surprise.

'Thank you for giving us a hand—' began Jim Pill.

'I didn't,' said the wizard. 'I was waiting at the other ground for you. What happened?'

Everyone stared at Stanley.

'Well, I thought if I said the wizard was there, you might play better,' he said. 'And you did!'

'Do you mean that we did all that playing ourselves?' asked Abesh. 'With no magic or anything?'

'That's right!'

'I can see you don't need me any more,' smiled the wizard, and vanished.

Blackbury United never saw the wizard again, but they did manage to win their League Cup that year.

Meanwhile, Real Caramba never discovered who had won the match for them. Stanley thought it best not to tell them – and he was probably right.

BEDWYR AND ARTHUR'S HILL

Half of this story you will believe is true, and half of the half you won't believe is unbelievable, but if you believe in it hard enough it will be truer.

Once upon a time – about a thousand years ago – there was a Welsh shepherd called Bedwyr. For most of the year he lived in the wild hills, but sometimes he used to drive his flock through England and sell them in London.

Bedwyr was the handsomest of all the shepherds, and his dog, Bedwetter, the finest sheepdog in all Wales.

Bedwyr knew this, and he was rather vain about it. In fact, one day when he was driving his flock before him, he thought, *With my handsome figure and my fine dog, all I need is a staff, and I'll be the greatest shepherd in all of Britain.*

So he stepped off the road and there, growing out of a small hillock, was a hazel tree. That should have made Bedwyr wary, because the hazel is an enchanted tree, and the wisest of all of them. But Bedwyr took his knife and cut a staff from it, then went on his way.

Bedwyr's staff proved to be pretty impressive. It was still unbroken and strong, even when all the other shepherds' staffs had split or broken. So, a few months after he'd found the hazel tree, Bedwyr took his flock to London, and made sure he took his trusty staff with him.

In those days London was like a big village, and after Bedwyr had sold his sheep he wandered round the markets, looking for a good inn at which to spend the night.

As he passed through the market, a little old man stepped out of the crowd and tapped him on the shoulder. The man was almost bent double, and something in his eyes made Bedwyr think he was very wise indeed.

'Young man, if you show me where you cut that stick, you will never lack for anything again. It is no ordinary staff. Notice how it has remained intact while all the other shepherds' staffs have broken.'

Bedwyr was a bit suspicious of this, but he promised the old man that if he met him outside the city gates in the morning, he would show him where he cut the stick.

So the next day Bedwyr and the Wise Man set off on the long road back to Wales. They travelled for many days until, not far from the valley of the River Severn, Bedwyr saw the hillock, and the hazel tree growing out of it.

'This is no ordinary tree, as I thought,' said the Wise Man, gesturing at its stump. Sure enough, at the point where Bedwyr had cut his staff, sap was still oozing – and it was pure gold. 'Dig this tree out of the ground, and you will lack for nothing,' he said.

'What is this hill?' asked Bedwyr, who, if truth were told, was beginning to get a little frightened.

'It is the hill under which King Arthur sleeps,' said the Wise Man. 'Now – **dig!** You will not regret it.'

Bedwyr started to dig up the hazel tree, while the Wise Man sat down on a rock and watched him. Soon, after much grunting and puffing, Bedwyr pulled the entire tree out of the ground. Under the roots was a round black hole.

'Very good,' said the Wise Man, and he jumped down the hole and disappeared. After hesitating for a moment or two, Bedwyr followed him and landed on a pile of dry grass. They were in a tunnel under the mound. Now Bedwyr was properly scared, but excited at the same time, and he let the Wise Man lead him along the tunnel until they turned a corner and came into a cave full of white light.

Bedwyr looked round in astonishment. In the cave, armed men and war horses lay sleeping, and the air was full of the sound of their breathing.

On a flat rock in the middle of the cave lay a warrior more finely dressed than the rest, with a long sword lying across his chest.

'This is where King Arthur sleeps,' said the Wise Man. 'Now that I have found him, you must be rewarded.'

He pointed to where a big bell hung from the

wall of the cave, a little way from the tunnel. On one side of it was a pile of gold, on the other a pile of silver.

'You may take all you can carry from one pile or the other, but on no account from both,' said the Wise Man.

So Bedwyr took off his coat and filled it full of gold coins. As he stood up he touched the bell with his elbow, and it gave a faint ring.

One of the sleeping warriors awoke and asked drowsily, 'Is it time?'

'Not yet,' said the Wise Man, and he hurried

the astonished Bedwyr out of the cave and back through the tunnel, where they clambered out of the mound.

There was enough gold to last the shepherd a lifetime, but he spent it all in a year and a day. So, plucking up his courage, Bedwyr went back into the mound.

Nothing had changed. But when he had filled his coat with silver coins this time, his shoulder touched the bell, and as its last note faded, several warriors rose to their feet.

'Are the Isles of Britain in danger?' they asked.

'No!' cried Bedwyr, and fled for his life.

But soon all his silver had been spent, and before long he found his way back to the mound for a third time.

'This is the last time I'll come,' he said, eyeing the sleeping warriors. But he filled his coat with gold and silver, and as he stood up he bumped his head on the bell.

And as it rang, the cave filled with the noise of waking men and horses.

Bedwyr dropped his coat and stood, petrified. But the Wise Man suddenly appeared between him and the knights.

'It is not time!' he cried. 'Would you awaken for this wretch?'

And he took Bedwyr by the ear and dragged him out of the mound.

'You nearly woke Arthur's knights – that would have been an absolute disaster!' he told Bedwyr. 'They must not ride forth until the day the great bell rings and the sky blackens, when the Isles of Britain will be threatened by a great enemy. And you disobeyed my warning,' he added. 'Not only will you never go back to Arthur's Hill, but for seven years and seven days all gold and silver you touch will turn to copper coins. That'll teach you not to meddle.'

With that, he vanished.

And, though he often tried, Bedwyr never again found his way back into Arthur's Hill.

MR TRAPCHEESE
AND HIS ARK

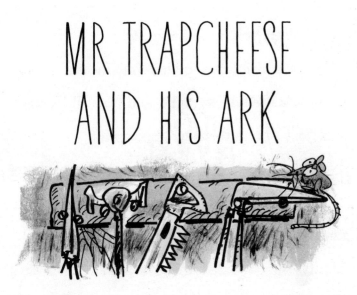

Old William Trapcheese was a carpenter in Dwindle-twixt-Waters, the little village just outside the proud old market town of Blackbury.

One day, he awoke in the middle of the night, pulled his trousers on and, lighting a candle – for Trapcheese was an old-fashioned man – he went down to his tool shed.

Next morning, his wife found him still there, measuring lengths of timber with his mouth full of nails.

'What are you up to there, Will?'

'I had a vision,' mumbled Trapcheese. 'I had a vision in a dream last night, and now all I know is that I must build this here contraption.'

Bertha Trapcheese looked at the odd contraption taking shape on the back lawn. 'Looks like a bit of a boat to me,' she said.

'Ah,' said Trapcheese, 'but what kind of a bit of a boat, eh? It's an ark, that is. It'll save you and me when the floods come. And the chickens, and the cat.'

'You mean like Noah's Ark?'

'Exactly. I had this dream. The waters covered the Earth. So I'm building an ark.'

Blimey! thought Bertha, and leaving her husband slowly sawing, she dashed off for the vicar.

The Reverend Gerald Flowerdew sat down on a pile of timber on the Trapcheeses' lawn. 'Now then, William,' he said. 'I understand you're building an ark.'

'That is correct,' said Trapcheese. 'I've been reading about Noah. Not hugely informative, but enough to get by.' He started measuring a piece of beechwood.

'I don't think the Bible was ever supposed to be a boatbuilding manual,' said Rev. Flowerdew. 'Er . . . when is the flood supposed to be coming?'

'August the twelfth, at noon,' said Mr Trapcheese. 'That's only a week ahead, so I'd be obliged if you'd get off that pile of wood there, and let me get on with it.'

By now news of Trapcheese's ark had spread around the village, and people had come out of their houses to see what all the fuss was about. The Mayor of Dwindle-twixt-Waters thought that the ark was a Planning Nuisance under Sub-section 33/B of the Town and

Country Malicious Lingering Act of 1821, and started a big debate in the Village Hall about it that went on all night. 'The man's a fool!' he said. 'We're in the middle of the hottest, driest spell of weather in living memory!'

William Trapcheese smiled to himself when he heard about this, and went on working, pausing only to grab a sandwich.

'The mayor's right – you are an old fool, William Trapcheese,' said his wife. 'Either you stop that there ark nonsense or I'm off!'

Mr Trapcheese thoughtfully hammered the stern deck of the ark into place. 'Well now,' he said, after a bit, 'I wouldn't like that.'

'Right then,' said Bertha triumphantly. 'So, you're going to stop?'

'No, I'm finishing this ark,' said Trapcheese determinedly.

Suffice to say, this did not go down well at all.

'You're a laughing stock, William Trapcheese!' were Bertha's last words before she stormed off.

Mr Trapcheese sighed and continued hammering.

But he was indeed a laughing stock.

When August the twelfth dawned bright and clear, people lined up along his fence and laughed. They even brought their lunches with them so they could have longer to laugh.

At half past eleven, Trapcheese put the last coat of paint on the finished ark. It stood like a giant toy on the lawn.

The sky was clear and blue.

Trapcheese lifted his dog, his four chickens and his two doves into the ark and climbed in after them, holding a picnic hamper.

He drank a cup of tea out of his Thermos flask and watched the crowd around the garden.

'Where's your umbrella, Trapcheese?' they shouted. 'Where's your wellies and your raincoat?'

Then at one minute to twelve a few white puffs of cloud came, and at noon it started to rain.

And it rained and it rained.

It soaked the people in the garden and streamed onto the roads. It ran over gutters and spurted out of gratings. In a few minutes the stream had overflowed, and the water levels in the town began to rise.

The village people, with Bertha in front, looked up at Trapcheese with pale faces. He put down his Thermos flask.

'Well now,' he said slowly. 'I reckon we've got room for one or two—'

He got no further.

Along the flooded path they squelched, and into the ark they tumbled, more and more of them, dragging suitcases and cows on ropes. They filled

the cabins and sat down on the deck and still more were running across the misty fields. And somehow Trapcheese and his animals got pushed overboard into the mud.

And at half past twelve, as he sat there all speckled with dirt, the sun came out.

The people on the ark looked down at Trapcheese.

The rain water gurgled away.

Trapcheese got up, brushed himself

down, opened a packet of custard cream biscuits and walked slowly off.

And they all heard him laughing and laughing and laughing.

DOGGINS HAS AN AWFULLY BIG ADVENTURE

Doggins walked along the seashore, while the wild westerly wind blew salt spray into his face. He always liked the sea, especially in spring, when it was green and mysterious. But Doggins was restless – he wanted an Awfully Big Adventure.

Far out to sea a great black bird was flying, but as it grew nearer Doggins saw that it was some sort of flying machine. He stared up as it landed on the sea, just beyond the beach. It had two large black wings and a cigar-shaped body, but instead of a tail it had a propeller and rudder. And where a bird's beak would have been was a large screw.

'Ahoy there!' shouted someone from the ship, opening a hatch. 'I say, it's Doggins! Fancy that!'

'Captain!' cried Doggins.

Yes, it was the captain he had flown with before on an airship, the world's greatest-ever explorer and inventor. With a surge of water the strange machine came right into the shore.

'Come aboard,' said the captain. He gestured to the ship. 'Like it? It's called the *Someone*, and it can go on land, sea and air.'

'Why call it *Someone*?' asked Doggins, as he clambered aboard.

'Well, I couldn't think of anyone to name it after,' explained the captain. 'I thought if I named it after someone particular, everyone else would be offended.'

Inside the *Someone*, Doggins' old friend, Ella, and a crewmate called Groundsel were playing dominoes, but they jumped up, delighted, when they saw Doggins. And when everyone had finished saying hello, Doggins asked the captain where he was exploring.

'Everywhere,' he said. 'A Big Adventure! You can come too, if you like.'

So when the *Someone* set off again, Doggins was a very happy member of the crew. The captain flooded the tanks, the ship sank below the sea's surface, and green water and bubbles floated past the portholes. A few inquisitive fish stared in at them.

It was very quiet under the sea.

'There's a very deep part of the sea called the Bottomless Canyon, where I thought we might go,' said the captain after a while. 'It's not far south.'

'How bottomless is it?' asked Doggins.

'Fantastically bottomless,' said the captain. 'Miles and miles deep. Black as coal, because no light gets down there.'

Little did the captain know that, far down in the Bottomless Canyon, was a little wooden box which was going to cause them a lot of trouble . . .

As the *Someone* got nearer to the Bottomless Canyon, schools of mer-people clustered around the portholes and waved to the crew inside, and striped fishes swam in crystal-clear water alongside them. Doggins was beginning to like underwater life.

'Bottomless Canyon ahead!' said the captain, at around teatime on the second day.

Underneath them, the ocean bed had disappeared, and there was nothing but rather wet-looking shadows.

'Doggins, switch on the lights! Groundsel, batten the laundry! Prepare to dive!' shouted the captain.

Down they went. Soon the brightly

coloured fish were left far behind. It was so dark that all the fish had lights of their own, which they carried on spikes at the end of their noses.

'We're miles and miles down now,' said the captain, looking at the dials.

They hit the bottom with a slight bump. All the lights went out. Ella started to look for the ship's fuse box, which would turn the lights back on.

'Don't look!' said Groundsel, who was hiding under his bunk. 'You never know what you might see!'

But when the captain switched on the lights they saw an enormous oyster! There were hundreds of them around the *Someone*, some with pearls the size of footballs.

'Just think,' said Doggins. 'A necklace of those would weigh tonnes!'

'You'd have to thread them on rope,' said the captain.

Groundsel crawled out, looking rather sheepish. 'Hey, look at that one!' he said.

Right by the *Someone* was an oyster the size of a house. As it opened they saw that inside, instead of a pearl, there was a small wooden box.

'Amazing,' said the captain. 'We must have a look at it!'

In the nose of the *Someone* was a sort of mechanical arm, and the captain was just able to snatch the box with it before the enormous oyster slammed shut again.

The box was about five centimetres square, and bound with brass. The captain put it on the table and, with great care, prised the lid open with a tiny screwdriver.

'There's nothing in there but a piece of paper,' said Ella.

And that was all it was. A tiny slip of yellow parchment. Across the top was written:

Frightened – weren't you!

'What bad manners!' exclaimed Groundsel.

There was more writing underneath.

'*This is the first box,*' read the captain. '*The second box is in the highest place in the world. Wear your woolly vests.*'

'How mysterious,' said Doggins.

'There's a bit more, right at the bottom,' said the captain. He showed it to them:

Puzzled – aren't you!

'Hmm,' said the captain. 'Mount Everest is the highest mountain in the world. Well, we'll have to go up there – let's get to the bottom of this!'

'The top, you mean,' said Doggins.

Soon the *Someone* rose to the surface and, wings flapping, took off for Mount Everest.

*

The *Someone* had been on the top of Mount Everest for three days, while the crew searched for the second box. All they had got was cold fingers. In the *Someone*'s stove was a fire built of Doggins' raincoat, three pairs of the captain's socks, Groundsel's stamp album and Ella's model of HMS *Victory* built out of matchsticks. They had burned everything else they had.

'It was a good stamp album,' sighed Groundsel.

Then someone knocked at the door.

When Doggins opened it, he saw a very small person standing in a puddle of melting snow. He was snow-white, hairy and bedraggled, and had large feet.

'Please,' said the creature, 'I am the Abominable Snowman and I am collecting for a new mattress. My old one's gone all lumpy.' Behind it the creature dragged a battered old mattress.

'It's the Abominable Snowman!' called out Doggins.

'He doesn't look very abominable,' said the captain.

The snowman looked a little put out at this, and blushed furiously.*

'He looks just bominable to me,' the captain added.

* Have you ever seen snow blush? No, I thought not. Me neither.

'My mattress is all lumpy,' the snowman said again, 'and I'm so very cold. All I have left in the world is this old wooden box, and it's not doing much to keep me warm.'

The captain and Doggins looked at each other, as they realized that *this* must be the second box! They dragged the bominable snowman inside and slammed the door.

'Funnily enough, Groundsel was just saying he'd like a lodger to live in his nice, warm left-hand overcoat pocket—'

'Was I?' said Groundsel.

'Yes,' said the captain firmly.

'Full board and lodging,' said Doggins, 'no visitors allowed after half-past ten.'

'Rent is one old box,' said Ella, who had finally cottoned on to the plan.

(Actually, Groundsel never regretted renting

his pocket to the bominable snowman, who was perfectly polite throughout his rather cosy stay, and never gave any trouble.)

The snowman agreed, and gave them the second box!

The captain levered the lid off with a tin opener. This time, the little piece of paper read:

Crafty – aren't you!

Then the captain read the rest aloud to the group: *'This is the second box. The third box is under Doggins' hat.'*

'It never is!' said Doggins, taking off his battered felt hat. A small wooden box fell out. 'It wasn't there a minute ago,' he said.

'I believe you, I believe you,' said the captain. 'This smells of magic.'

Inside the box was another message – they all crowded round to read it:

Flabbergasted – aren't you!

Staggered – aren't you!

And then, right at the bottom of the page, was the message:

Box Number Four is Lost and Found

'Lost and Found,' said the captain.

'Hmm. Maybe it means at a Lost Property Office?
But the nearest is thousands of miles away.'

'What's property?' asked the snowman.

'Your mattress and my hat,' said Doggins.

The captain muttered and went outside to start
the engines.

A few minutes later the *Someone* took off out of
the snowdrift and flapped into the cold sky. Doggins
put the boxes on the fire, and they disappeared in
two green flashes.

'I don't like this,' said the captain. 'Still, what
can go wrong at a Lost Property Office?'

*

After a few weeks of travelling, the *Someone* finally arrived at the nearest Lost Property Office (which happened to be not-so-conveniently placed in London).

They landed in a big park in the middle of the city, and the five explorers climbed the steps to the

Lost Property Office, which was in a big building with marble pillars outside.

'Boxes?' said the man behind the counter, who looked as if he was rather lost himself. 'We've got all sorts – big ones, small ones, cardboard ones—'

'This one is wooden,' interrupted the captain.

The man stared nervously at the bominable snowman, who was eating an ice cream. 'I'll just go and look,' he said.

He disappeared into a pile of abandoned suitcases. Doggins and the others sat around waiting.

'No wooden boxes of any description,' he said, coming back, 'except this one. It's been here for hundreds of years.'

'That's it!' said the captain. He grabbed the box and they all ran from the building.

'Now wait just one second!' shouted the Lost Property man. 'You can't just run off with that. I'll have the law on you!'

When they got back to the *Someone*, breathless, Groundsel prised the fourth box open with his penknife. Inside was the usual slip of paper:

Surprised – aren't you!

'Well, not any more,' said Doggins.

It went on:

This is the last clue. Everything will be explained if you find the furthermost island. Good luck.

'Get the atlas, Ella,' said the captain.

'Hmm. Furthermost,' said Ella, as she laid the atlas out and studied it. 'Furthermost from where?'

There was a high whistling noise.

'Duck!'

shouted Groundsel.

A black arrow burst through the porthole and shuddered into the wall! It was covered in ice, as though it had been flying a long way at a very great height.

'Thundering grouts!'*

said the captain.

There was a message tied onto the arrow. It said:

Everywhere

---

* These are rather like the thunderous noises that can come from someone who has just eaten a big plateful of Brussels sprouts, but a lot *lot* louder. So beware.

'This positively reeks of magic,' said Doggins.*

'I think I've found it,' said the captain, pointing.

There on the atlas was a tiny speck, miles from any nearby islands, and many miles from London. It was all by itself in the middle of the ocean.

'Oh, I see,' said Doggins. 'So you think this is the Furthermost Island because it's the one furthest away from any other islands? That's clever.'

'That's right,' said the captain. 'And I don't mind telling you, I am positively boiling with righteous indignation! No one shoots arrows at me – even magical ones. We are going to end this mad treasure hunt once and for all!'

'I'm full of righteous indignation too,' said Groundsel, but no one seemed to hear him.

* Better than reeking of Brussels sprouts, anyway.

*

So, not long after, the *Someone*
was flying at top speed over the ocean. There was
a dot on the horizon which grew bigger and bigger,
with sea-lashed cliffs and forbidding mountains
coming into focus as they drew nearer.

'Right,' said the captain. 'Now we shall see.'

Ella brought the *Someone* down in a wood
of old black trees. Gusts of wind bowled around,
and heavy grey clouds seemed so low you could
touch them.

After locking up the *Someone* securely,
and buttoning up their raincoats, the five
explorers squelched nervously between
the dripping trees. Every now and again
something howled mournfully, and a low

rumbling could be heard in the distance.

'About now,' said the captain, with rain dripping off his coat and into his shirt collar, 'something should happen.'

Everyone looked around nervously. Groundsel sneezed, and Doggins took out his handkerchief to blow his nose . . .

And saw, embroidered on his hand-kerchief in red, white and blue silk, the words:

Follow the arrows!

The explorers looked around, and saw a red arrow nailed to a tree.

'It's bound to be a trap,' said the captain. 'But we need to find out who's at the bottom of all this!'

So they followed the arrows along a winding path, across bottomless ravines on narrow bridges, and past big black rocks balanced precariously atop ledges, ready to fall at a moment's notice.

As they got further into Furthermost Island, the five explorers could see a high mountain at its centre – black as coal and with sides as smooth as ice. On the very top of it was what looked like a stone tower, windswept and lonely.

Doggins and the rest of the crew wound round and round the mountain, following the trail of arrows. Various magical things kept happening. The captain found a rubber snake in his hat. Groundsel's boots turned to cheese. Ella's fountain pen grew wings and flew into a pear tree, where it perched, singing. But the bold explorers were getting used to this sort of thing.

'Untoward happenings deter us not,' said the captain, as his trousers turned blue. 'This seems to be a place of natural magic,' he added. 'Natural magic can grow in certain places, like coconuts or rice.'

'Eh?' said the bominable snowman.

'What I mean,' said the captain patiently, 'is that in most places everything you do causes something you can expect. If you throw a stone in the air, it comes down again; and if you plant an acorn, it grows into an oak tree. But in some places, like this island, everything gets mixed up. You can never be sure your acorn won't turn into sealing wax—'

'Or cabbages or kings,' said Groundsel.

'Or a trolleybus,' said Ella.

'Or a hive of bees,' said Doggins.

'Exactly,' said the captain.

While they were talking they had come to the tower. So the captain knocked on the big wooden door. But instead of making a knocking sound, his fist made a ringing noise.

'You see?' said the captain. 'You never know what might happen.'

'Come in,' said a voice, as the door creaked open. 'I have been expecting you.'

The five intrepid explorers stood nervously at the door of the tower, wondering whether they should run away. It didn't help matters when a bit of stray magic brushed against Doggins' hat and turned it into cardboard.

Then a woman stepped out. The tip of her hat was way above their heads, and she wore a rather grubby blue robe. Her hair was bright yellow and bushy, so she looked like someone peering out of a dandelion.

All in all, she looked rather grand, and very magical. In a voice that sparkled, she said, 'I am The Enchantress.'

'Er, good afternoon,' said the captain. 'We've come about the boxes.'

'Capital, capital!' cried the enchantress. 'Come on in and tell me all about it.'

And because there didn't seem anything better to do, and the enchantress didn't look too menacing or dangerous,* they followed her into the tower.

They walked down a corridor full of the most unusual junk and clutter. Rubber snakes and wire spiders hung from the walls. There were boxes full of red noses and false beards. Flowers which squirted water when they were pressed hung from pots in the ceiling. Books were everywhere.

'You'll have to excuse the mess,' said the

enchantress. 'I've been working on a new joke.' She stopped when they reached what appeared to be a main hall, but it was stuffed so full of rubbish (clowns' feet here, a wand there, a dinosaur costume hanging from the chandelier), it was difficult to tell.

'So, I expect you're wondering why I left all those clues in boxes,' she said, as they shuffled round, looking for places to sit. 'Well, I need a bit of help. I'm a Joke Wizard, you see.'

'Eh?' said Groundsel.

'I make up jokes. And surprises. I bury treasure for people to find and

* Though Groundsel was just a *little* bit scared
of dandelions, so had to hide behind Ella as
they went through the door.

put ghosts in haunted houses. I invent things to stop people getting bored.'

Every joke ever told was made up by her, the enchantress explained. But she'd run out . . . It was years since she'd invented a new joke, and people had nothing to laugh at. The last original joke was sealed inside a mountain, but it could only be used on the very last day of the world. In the meantime people would just get more and more serious.

'So I thought, whoever could find all the boxes – and you need a special kind of mind to work out all the clues – would be just the person to help,' she finished, looking at them meaningfully.

'Well,' said the captain, 'do you know the one about the three bananas?'

'Yes.'

'Or the one about the magic nails?' asked Groundsel.

'Yes.'

'What about,' said Doggins, 'the one about the cat's pyjamas? There was this cat, and it only wore purple pyjamas . . .'

And so Doggins went on for a full ten minutes, telling the joke about the cat and the purple pyjamas, until he finished with, 'So the grocer said: "All right, but that's a funny way to eat lettuce!"' Everyone was in hysterics. Even the enchantress was laughing, and the bominable snowman had to have his head held under the tap (he'd overheated because he'd been laughing so hard).

'Capital!' said the enchantress, and she offered Doggins a job on the spot.

So when the *Someone* left the following morning, Doggins stayed behind, and is probably still making up jokes to this day.

But the one about the cat's pyjamas is still a mystery to me.

JOHNNO, THE TALKING HORSE

Mr Sid Ferret, the last scrap dealer in the market town of Blackbury to drive a horse and cart, got up early one fine Monday morning to feed his horse. It was while he was adjusting the nosebag that a muffled voice said:

'A fine morning.'

'**Fine,**' said Sid, looking round to see who had come into the stable.

'It was me what said that,' said Johnno, the horse, in a reproachful voice.

Now Sid Ferret was a lot of things that aren't generally approved of in polite circles. He had a bath only when he felt like it, for one thing – living alone as he did – and some mornings he used to sleep in till all hours. He had also been known to drink his tea from the saucer. But one thing he wasn't, and that was a fool. If a horse talked to Sid Ferret, he didn't sit down and start trying to make out he hadn't heard anything.

'**Well, well, well, well,**' he said. '**How long have you been able to talk?**'

'Oh, ages,' said Johnno, swinging his tail.

'You said "A fine morning",' said Sid. 'I've never heard you say that before.'

'It's usually been a pretty rotten morning until now,' said Johnno.

'Um,' said Sid.

He left Johnno chomping on his breakfast and strolled back indoors. Some people would have rung up a zoo or a circus. Not Sid. Ever tried telephoning a zoo and saying you've got a talking horse? It's very difficult to get people to listen.

Sid fried himself some bread and thought about it. Then he went back to the stable.

'We're going on our rounds then?' he asked.

'Aha,' said Johnno. 'When you thought I couldn't talk, it was just on with the old horse collar, into the old shafts and off we jolly well go, wasn't it? Bit more civil now, aren't we? Bit more respect shown, eh? Not so much of the old *hey-up* and *whoa* now, eh? Yes, all right. Let's try the Mafeking Road area. We haven't done that for a long time.'

Mafeking Road and the surrounding streets did produce quite a lot of good scrap, so they loaded up the cart, then found a quiet lay-by and Johnno had a nosebag while Sid had tea out of a flask and read the paper.

'Horse races,' he said, reading the racing pages. 'You interested at all, Johnno?'

'No. Hunting, now. I'd like that. Come to think of it, I want to go *fox*-hunting. My dad used to hunt foxes. If I can't go hunting, I'll go on strike.'

'Fox-hunting!' gasped Sid. 'But that's posh! And not like your dad's day, you know – most hunts nowadays don't chase real foxes.' He gulped. **'And I can't ride!'**

'Oh well, as to riding, I'll see to that. But being as I'm a partner at this firm, with never a decent wage – hunting it's got to be!'

*

Sid joined the Blackbury Hunt. It cost him a lot of money, especially when he had to buy a special jacket and long boots.

'That's not all,' he said, when he came back to the house. 'I've still got a saddle to buy before next Saturday.'

'Won't need one, mate,' said Johnno, who was eating the lawn. 'I'll see to it you don't fall off. Just so long as they don't have any dogs there. I hate perishing dogs.'

'Um, I think they have one or two foxhounds,' said Sid s l o w l y.

'Huh,' sneered Johnno.

On Saturday – and much against his better judgement – Sid dressed up in his new hunting jacket and led Johnno out of the stable.

By the time they got to the meeting place at the Jug and Bottle Sid was getting quite used to riding.*

* He had also taken the precaution of wearing *very thick* underpants to protect his bottom.

There were a lot of other people on horseback, drinking little drinks, and when the man came and asked Sid what he wanted he said, 'A brown ale.'

'And I'll have a pale ale, in a pail,' growled Johnno. 'And there's too many rotten dogs around.'

'Blimey!' said the man.

The other huntsmen were looking rather oddly at Sid, perhaps because he had left his flat cap on and his horse did not even have a saddle. But at last the hunt rode off down a lane.

A horn sounded from a nearby wood. And before anyone could move, Johnno had bunched his legs together and was off like a rocket, closely followed by the foxhounds.

'Yoicks!' shouted Johnno.

! thought Sid.

The Blackbury Hunt streamed across the fields. Slightly in the lead was a desperate fox, which had got in the way of the hunters. The fox was followed by the hounds, which were closely followed by Johnno the cart horse – with Sid Ferret hanging on for dear life.

'Too many rotten dogs,' **hissed** Johnno, thundering through the yelping pack. 'I wouldn't give you tuppence for a dog!'

'You're not supposed to kick them,' screamed Sid. Far behind him he could hear the other huntsmen shouting and swearing.

Slowly Johnno drew level with the fox.

'What happens now?' he said. 'Do we get a prize or something for catching Mister Fox up?' He turned round and bared his big teeth at the nearest hound, which was racing across the field behind them and had nearly caught them up.

Sid Ferret managed to pant out what could happen to the fox if the dogs reached it.

'Never!' swore Johnno. 'Catch me standing by while a lot of perishing dogs – here, you, small change, yes, you with the lollopy tongue, making all that silly noise: *I don't like dogs!'*

Perhaps it was only a coincidence, but with one great bound the fox leaped up and fell onto Johnno's neck. It looked sideways at Sid and growled.

With a horse laugh, Johnno pounded on, sailing over streams and hedges while the fox clung onto his mane. Far behind him the Master of Foxhounds, Lord Cake, had already gone red with rage,* and now his rage was making him turn purple with fury.

'I'm enjoying this,' said Johnno. 'But personally I could do with another nice cold beer.'

'You're a horse,' said Sid, as they trotted down the lonely lane. 'Horses are supposed to drink water. And you've had one pail of beer already!'

But Johnno resolutely turned into the courtyard of a small pub and snorted. 'A *pail* ale, please, and I expect the fox would like a packet of chicken-flavoured crisps,' he said.

Sid Ferret sighed. He was beginning to wish

* So red, like a tomato, that his face actually matched his posh jacket.

Johnno had never learned to talk.

A few minutes later he came back with the pail of ale and the crisps. But Johnno and the fox had gone.

Sid stood in the middle of the lane in his torn and muddy hunting outfit and stared around.

Sid Ferret was trudging up the lane, looking for Johnno, when he heard the distant strains of music and cheering. It sounded like a fair. He tramped towards the sound, and came to a field that held a few roundabouts and sideshows surrounding a circus tent.

Then, as a big roundabout turned slowly, he saw Johnno and the fox. The horse was standing among the gilded hobby horses on the round-about – and was holding the roundabout attend-ant by the seat of his trousers.

'Fifteen pence a go!' the horse was muttering,

through great yellow teeth. 'Daylight robbery! I'll report you!'

'Put him down this minute!'

bellowed Sid, dashing towards the roundabout.

'Fifteen times this brute's been round,' growled the attendant, 'to say nothing of assault and wear and tear on my trousers!'

Sid sighed, took out his wallet and the last of his savings, and handed the man a bundle of notes.

'This is another fine mess you've got me into, Johnno,' he said. 'Have you got any more plans? You wouldn't like a go on the helter-skelter?'

'Don't be sarky,' said the horse.

Just then the circus ringmaster ran up and offered Sid a big cigar.

'Amazing ventriloquism, that,' he said. 'You make it sound like that bag of bones is really talking.'

'What's all this about a bag of bones?' asked Johnno, with a yellow glint in his eye.

'He really talks,' said Sid, 'and if I were you, I'd guard my tongue. Come on, Johnno, let's go home.'

'Hey, no,' said the ringmaster. 'This is great! He really talks, eh? Just what we need! How'd you like to join the circus? Both of you and – er – that fox you've got on your back . . .'

'I don't think—' began Sid.

'We're pleased to accept,' said Johnno. 'When do we start?'

The ringmaster, whose name was Mr Rose, gave them three seats for that night's performance so they could see what they were letting themselves in for.

'It says here the first act is Elvira Madigan and her Amazing Dancing Horse,' said Sid, who had a programme. *Oh dear*, he thought. *I've a feeling there's going to be trouble.*

Sid and Johnno the talking horse sat watching as the circus act came on. 'Elvira and her Amazing Dancing Horse' turned out to be a rather beautiful young girl on a very pretty young mare with a silvery coat.

'Wellwellwellwellwell,' said Sid and Johnno together. 'What a good-looking girl!'

There was a lot of leaping through hoops and standing on upturned barrels by Elvira and her horse, and then, when they left the ring to tumultuous applause – Johnno clapped by banging his hooves together – the clowns came on.

It was while they were capering about that Johnno leaned over to Sid and said, 'I can smell smoke.'

Sid turned round and saw smoke coming under the flap of the big top. 'There's a fire,' he whispered. 'Now, we must keep a cool head . . .'

'Oh, quite,' said Johnno. He raised his great head and neighed: **'FIIIRRRRRE!'**

There was, of course, instant confusion. It turned out later that the ringmaster had thrown his cigar away into a pile of straw. Flames leaped up and were soon roaring from tent to tent, while the audience and the circus people dashed around in the smoke. There was a terrified neighing from the tent where the horses were kept, which was already ablaze.

Sid seized a bucket of water from a passing clown and clambered onto Johnno's back.

'That lovely little grey mare might be in there,' muttered Johnno, as he galloped through the flames and burning straw with Sid pouring water out of the bucket onto the fires. Guided by the neighing, they found the horses. The mare was there – and so was Elvira, who was trying to calm all the horses.

Ever the gentleman, Sid raised his cap, which was already smouldering, and said, 'Good evening, madam. If you'll kindly get in line behind me I think we'll be all right.'

Johnno roared horsy commands at the frightened horses, and a few minutes later he led them in an orderly fashion to safety, just as the tent crashed down behind them in a shower of sparks.

'I don't know how to thank you—' began Elvira.

'Well, they do a very nice meal at the Blackbury Arms, so how about riding over there with me?' said Sid.

So they did, for two rounds of steak and chips and a couple of nosebags and a pail of ale for Johnno and the silvery mare, who stayed out in the yard.* And Johnno and Sid then joined the circus and left Blackbury for ever, except for the occasional visit.

Everyone got married, of course – after all, why not?

---

*The fox got another packet of chicken-flavoured crisps, which he shared with a very pretty young vixen he met behind the bins.

THE WILD KNIGHT

Before I tell you the story of the Wild Knight, I'd better explain how Henry Stump came to be Sir Henry Stump.

He left school aged ten with nothing more in his pocket than three marbles, a sixpence with a hole in it, a used bus ticket to East Slate and his hands – he was a very lazy boy.

But he sold the ticket to a used-bus-ticket collector, sold his sixpence to a rare sixpence dealer, played marbles so well that he won three thousand more (which he sold at a toy shop), and used his hands to collect the money to go to a shop and buy himself a new suit.

With clean clothes and a bit of imagination there's no stopping anyone, and our story opens when middle-aged Henry Stump was one of the richest men in Gritshire.

Rupert Vest, Stump's chauffeur, was sitting in the car outside Buckingham Palace with Daphne, Henry Stump's daughter. They were waiting for *Sir* Henry Stump to come out. This was the great day when he would be knighted – for being rich and successful and a very good businessman.

The short fat figure of Sir Henry Stump waddled down the palace steps, rubbing his shoulders where the knighting sword had been a bit heavy. Beside him walked Lord Featherdown, his best friend. Lord Featherdown wasn't a very rich man, in spite of being a lord; but he was the sort of person who *looked* as if he was a very rich man.

'Well, Daddy,' said Daphne, as they got into the car. 'What are you going to do now you're a sir?'

'Congratulations, sir,' said young Rupert Vest, starting the car.

'My braces feel sawn through by that sword,' said Sir Henry, and left it at that. But while they were driving back to Gritshire his mind was working very fast. Because, you see, Sir Henry was a very careful man.

When he became a factory owner, he made sure he knew how to be a proper factory owner.

If he bought, say, a steel mill, he was always careful to know how steel mills should be run.

The question now was: What did a knight actually *do*?

That evening, when the two of them were sitting in the study, he asked Featherdown.

'I really don't know,' said His Lordship. 'I don't

suppose there's much call for jousting, fighting dragons, rescuing damsels and whatnot these days.'

'Hmm,' said Sir Henry thoughtfully.

That night he took a book from his library and read all about knights. All about jousting, and fighting dragons, and rescuing damsels and going on quests. The more he read, the more he began to look forward to getting down to the job – if this was what knights did, he was jolly well going to do it now.*

Next morning, when the butler came to bring him breakfast in bed, Sir Henry was gone.

But there was a great commotion down in the village . . .

The village policeman cycled up to Stump Hall, and everyone decided to meet in the library. The

---

* It also sounded like a lot of fun.

only one missing was Sir Henry himself – no one knew where he had got to.

'It seems that someone took Fred Mundles' cart horse from its stable last night,' said Crampon, the policeman, 'and left a cheque for five hundred pounds pinned to the door.'

'That's Daddy, all right,' sighed Daphne. 'Only he would think that Mundles' moth-eaten old bonebag is worth that much. What is Mundles going to do?'

'I think he's quite happy,' said Crampon. 'There's been no crime committed, as far as he's concerned. I just thought I'd better tell you.'

Well, it had started.

First the cart horse was taken.

Then, a bit later, Lord Featherdown sent a note round to say that someone had broken into his house and stolen a short fat suit of armour and a long thin sword. 'I'm not worried about the armour – glad to see it go, in fact – but I'm afraid Sir Henry might do himself a mischief with that sword.'

'Tell me,' said Rupert Vest slowly, after he had read the note. 'Can your dad use a sword?'

'Actually, it's news to me that he can even ride a horse,' said Daphne.

'What's occupying my mind now is what he thinks he is going to use the sword on,' said Rupert. They looked at each other for a moment. Then: **'I'll start the car. Quick! No time to lose!'** shouted Rupert, as he ran to the garage.

A minute later they had picked up Lord Featherdown and shot out of the village.

'I found this book open in his study,' said Daphne. 'Daddy's underlined some of the writing.' The book was called *Knights of Old*. 'Everyone keep a lookout,' said Daphne. 'It says here . . . "The knights would keep the law and right wrongs" – Rupert, put the car radio on. You never know.'

Click . . .

'And reports are still coming in about this strange knight, last seen near Blackbury. A police description says that he is short, fat and mounted on a cart horse. So far he has cut down all the parking meters in the town centre, held up a Snowy White Cut-Price Washo van, and somehow managed to sink Big B, the pirate radio station moored on a raft in Blackbury reservoir. (Hee-hee! Ha-ha-ha! Ho-ho.) This is the BBC Home Service (Ha-ha ha! Gluggle! That's showing 'em) . . .'

Click!

'Well, I liked Big B,' said Daphne defiantly, 'even if Daddy hated it. We've got to find him quickly!'

'The trouble is, there's no room for knights these days,' muttered Lord Featherdown.

Lord Featherdown was right. There *was* no room for knights these days.

Sir Henry Stump guided his old cart horse along the side of the Blackbury–London motorway, his rusty sword hanging by his side. Cars honked at him as they rushed by. *I bet Sir Lancelot didn't get honked at*, he thought.

It was a strange sort of day, very hot and yellowy, and every now and again thunder rumbled in the distance. Anyone who was watching might have seen what looked like a green mist suddenly appear on top of a hill overlooking the roadway – but no one *was* watching. The mist cleared, and atop the small hill three figures sat on horseback.

One was a tall knight in black and gold armour,

mounted on a snorting black stallion.

The man in the middle wore a high golden crown, and shining white armour. At his side was a long sword.

The third person was concentrating very hard, because he was in the middle of a difficult spell. He looked like a wizard, in his tall purple hat and flowing beard, with a long robe covered with mystic signs.

'I should hurry up, sire,' he muttered. 'I don't think I can hold this spell much longer. Time-travelling is not my cup of mead.'

'Well,' said the proud king. 'What do you think, Sir Lancelot?'

'I don't know,' said the black knight. 'It makes a change to find someone who still believes in us. Give him a trial, sire, see if he is a true knight. Give him the test.'

'Spotted, green or flame-throwing?' said Merlin.

'Flame-throwing,' said the king.

They watched Sir Henry as he rode sadly along the road. Then, as the wizard said the magic words, two things happened:

The car containing Rupert Vest, Daphne Stump and Lord Featherdown screeched to a halt alongside Sir Henry.

And a dragon suddenly appeared in front of the car, rolling its eyes and breathing fire.

'Oh dear,' said Lord Featherdown, and fainted.

But something rushed past them, straight at the dragon, drawing a rusty sword.

'He'll do, sire. He's brave enough,' said Sir Lancelot. 'Now I'd better get down there before that dragon kills him.'

'No need,' smiled the king.

For Sir Henry had killed the dragon. He stood

by it, wondering what on earth had happened, and then the three horsemen rode down to him. After the man with the crown had said something to him, Sir Henry waved his hand at the people in the car. Still waving, he rode back up the hill after the knights . . . and was gone in the magic mist.

'Do you think we'll ever see him again?' said Daphne later, when the three of them sat in the library.

'Who knows?' said Rupert. 'Did you notice, when he left, there was a sound like many horses riding by after him? And on the hill, before the mist closed, I thought there was a sort of castle . . .'

'I think he'll be all right,' said Lord Featherdown quietly. He showed them the book that Sir Henry had been reading. On one page there was a small picture of Camelot, and King Arthur was shown watching a tournament.

'Look by King Arthur's left shoulder,' said Lord Featherdown.

They looked.

There, next to the wizard Merlin and Sir Lancelot, was a very small knight in rusty armour, smiling all over his face . . .

THE WERGS' INVASION OF EARTH

It was the best of voyages. It was the worst of voyages. Now, far above the Earth hung the Wergs' flying saucer, spinning slowly. The captain of the Wergs, One, peered down.

'Not bad at all,' he said. 'The inhabitants are pretty stupid, you know. We should conquer them in a brace of shakes.'

'I've picked up their television signals,' said Three. All the Wergs gathered round the screen.

'Ugh! Aren't they hairy?' said Two.

'Hardly out of the caves,' agreed One.

'They look quite like us,' said Three, 'only much bigger.'

'On the surface,' said One. 'Gentlewergs, this is far too good a planet to be left to those creatures. But it's just right for us. We'll land on the night side, and this time tomorrow the planet will be ours.'

'I hope it's worth coming all these light-years for,' whispered Two to Three.

A few minutes later the saucer landed. If anyone had been listening – no one was – they would have heard a small door hiss open.

'High-frequency rifles at the ready,' said One. 'We are in a wood. Remember, there are still wild creatures on this planet. Two, Three, Four and Five, come with me.'

The five Wergs stepped out of the saucer and crept through the darkness.

'We saw the lights of a city to the east as we landed,' whispered Three.

Then the bushes parted, and a big grey creature hurled itself at the five invaders. **Wump!** went the guns, and it rolled over in the dust.

'What a monster!' said Four. 'Look at its teeth – and that tail!'

But there was still a rustling in the trees.

'Stand ready to fire again,' said One.

Then they saw it. Two green eyes staring like lamps, whiskers twitching, giant paws sheathed with long claws; a great creature peered down at the trembling Wergs.

'*Miaow!*' it said.

'F-fire,' gasped One.

Wump!

The cat didn't seem to notice. It sat down and stared at them. And at its lunch, which the Wergs had helpfully shot for it.*

'When I say run, run,' said One.

'Run!'

Two crept out from behind a stone, and felt for bruises. The great eyes of the cat were nowhere to be seen – nor were the other Wergs. He shivered.

'One?' he called out. 'Three, are you there? Where are you, Four? F-F-Five?'

There was no reply. Had the giant cat got them?

Two spent the rest of the night in a bush. He wondered whether the others had found their way back to the flying saucer when they ran from the cat. Perhaps they thought he had been caught –

---

* The main course, anyway. For now that they had its attention, the cat was wondering if the Wergs might make a nice tasty snack to follow the mouse.

they might have taken off without him! It was with cheerful thoughts like these that the little Werg kept himself awake all night.

The rising sun found him tramping through the grass. Sometimes he stopped and called out, but no one answered. Dew soaked his suit, and he was feeling extremely hungry.

Then ahead of him he saw a palace, bigger even than the one belonging to Billion, Lord of the Wergs. It was made of bricks. Each one would have taken the strength of a hundred Wergs to lift it.

This must be slaves, thought Two. *That means they can't be very civilized. I shall amaze them with my superior intelligence. That's what I shall do.* And perhaps, he thought, one of the other Wergs had found his way there already.

He crept into the house – there was enough room for him to crawl under the door – and at once his sensitive nose caught the smell of food. Wide-eyed, he wandered past gigantic furniture and found his way to the pantry. Food! He could see it on shelves high above him, tantalizing him with delicious smells. But he couldn't reach it.

While he stood there he heard a squeak, and turning round he saw a large grey creature, just like the one the cat had chased towards them. This one was caught in a steel box.

Two turned a dial on a translator machine attached to his belt, and became the first Werg to hear a mouse speak.

'Help! Get me out of this! Press that little button on the back of the box and the door will open.'

This must be an Earthman, thought Two. He went round the back of the trap and found the button. The door sprang open.

'Thank you,' said the mouse.

'Don't mention it,' squeaked Two. 'Er – take me to your leader. Or your larder.'

The mouse led Two to a hole in the larder wall.

'Are you the chief race on Earth, then?' asked the Werg. 'I – we, that is – we thought those in charge looked more like us.'

The mouse put its head on one side. 'You won't find a place on Earth without us, or our cousins the rats,' it said. 'We get everywhere. Of course there are cats, and things called men – who do look a bit like you – but they don't count.'

'Why not?'

'You'll have to ask our leader that. Really, all men do is feed us and house us. They're just great boobies with no brains at all.'

'Hmm,' said Two thoughtfully. If only he hadn't lost his gun when the cat chased him! This mouse-creature looked pretty weak and he might need to defend both of them.

The mouse led him along a tunnel to a cave gnawed out behind the pantry. It was full of torn-up newspaper and smelled strongly of cheese. *What a shambles*, thought Two. If only he could contact the flying saucer . . .

Sitting in the centre of the mouse hole was a great fat mouse, whose hair was almost white. Others sat round him, and set up an excited squeaking when Two entered.

Two found it very difficult to explain space travel to the mice.

'You look very much like the big men,' said the chief mouse. 'They lay traps for us, and set cats on us. But for all that,' he went on, 'we'll be here after they've gone, just as we were here before they came. They make food which we eat, and work

while we sleep. We mice are the most civilized race on Earth.'

'I see. Well, sir, if you will send some of your – er – mice to escort me back to my – er – my machine, I think we have something there which will help you fight cats and men. Our only aim is to establish peace between Wergs and mice,' said Two.

So three of them hurried out of the hole with him and made their way through the garden. Of course, Two had no intention of helping the mice. *These men sound even more stupid than the mice,* he thought – *we'll be able to take over the whole planet! They might even make me Dictator!*

'I smell cat,' said one of the mice.

'Hmm?' asked Two, his mind busy with schemes and plans. Then, just as he saw the outline of the Wergs' saucer only a little way off, there was a rustling behind him.

It was the cat again!

The two mice squeaked and scampered away, leaving Two all alone. He heard a loud purring behind him, and ran for his life.

There's the saucer! he thought. *I hope it's cat-proof!* He reached it and started banging frantically on the airlock door. It was opened by One.

'Oh, it's you—' One began. Then he saw the cat, which was watching the saucer with interest. **'Gah!'** said One, and slammed the door shut again, leaving Two cowering against the airlock.

He could hear the interplanetary motors inside start up. The ground under the saucer began to glow with an electric blue light, and the cat blinked sleepily.

It put out a paw and carelessly flipped the Wergs' best exploration and conquest ship over.

Two peered out cautiously from the grass where

he had hidden, to see the great furry creature turning the saucer over and over between its paws. A smile crossed his green face. He thought of the big fat pompous One tumbling upside down . . .

'What an unWergian thought,' he said out loud, surprised at himself. 'Supposing we never get away. Then other Wergs will come and not find out about this terrible planet until too late! 'Tis a far, far Wergian thing I do now than I have ever done before.' And thinking of the great Wergs of history, Two cut himself a length of sharp grass and dashed at the cat.

Jab! Jab! The cat dropped the saucer and peered down at the defiant Werg. There was a high-pitched whine, and a flash of light, and the saucer zoomed skywards.

Two watched it go and turned to the cat, who was very surprised to see a mouse with a sting. It backed away, and Two jabbed at it again. Then the cat drew itself together and walked off haughtily, waving its tail.

Left behind, thought Two. *That's me. All alone. Marooned. All by myself. A solitary castaway. Oh well, it can't be helped.*

He thought of the great space empire of the Wergs, and the thousands of planets under their control. No more of that. No more conquering. It actually didn't seem too bad to be all alone on Earth.

So Two, the castaway Werg, started his wandering life. It's easy to steal a ride when you are only an inch high – under the tarpaulins of a long-distance lorry, in the galleys of ships, in the luggage compartments of jets.

He's been to London and New York, hunted angel fish in coral reefs and now – well, he could be anywhere.

BASON AND THE HUGONAUTS

Once upon a time there was a man named Jason who, with a band of men called the Argonauts, sailed to the end of the world to steal the Magic Golden Fleece. You may have heard of him – it's a very well-known story.

Not half so well-known is the story of Bason and the Hugonauts who, about the same time as Jason, set out themselves to find the Tin Fleece.

You see, Bason lived in Tropnecia, a tiny island all by itself in the Mediterranean, and one day the king of that land – Plous by name – heard about an island a long way off where there was a lot of tin.

Of course, he knew that once anyone sailed out of the Mediterranean they were more than likely to fall off the edge of the world, since Plous was an educated man and knew that the world was flat.

Still, tin – pretty useful thing, he thought. *I know – I'll send Bason. He's brave and strong and perhaps he doesn't know about falling over the edge of the world.*

So he sent for Bason. Now Bason was a fisherman, who lived in a hut by the shore, and he was very amazed when the king sent for him. He was even more amazed when the king said:

'Ah, Bason, just the man I want to see. Look

here, I gather that there's this island that's full of tin and sheep, just out of the Mediterranean, turn right and keep straight on. I've heard there's a Tin Fleece. Take a boat and bring it back, will you? Take a few friends. Make a holiday of it.'

'But why me, sire?' asked Bason.

'Um? Oh, we think you're the dependable sort who can be relied upon,' said Plous airily. 'Take old Hugo the boat-builder. Take Nautilus, the inventor. Take anyone you want. Oh, and there's something else . . .' And he signalled to the guards. They brought in a small hairy bundle which, Bason saw, was chained hand and foot.

'This – thing is one of the people who live there,' said Plous. 'Ugly brute, isn't he? Washed up last night in a very odd little boat. You might as well take him. He's either covered in blue paint or he just looks like that anyway.'

So they handed the hairy man's chain to Bason and hurried him out of the palace. Plous was pleased. You see, he knew that Bason was deeply in love with his daughter, Eriden, and Plous didn't approve. Half the fish that Bason sent to the palace were full of little notes, for one thing, and for another, Plous didn't want a common fisherman for a son-in-law.

In fact, if Bason ever managed to return . . . But Plous was pretty sure he wouldn't.

Bason led the hairy man down to the harbour and called his friends together.

'Apparently there's this island full of tin sheep, according to Plous,' he told them. 'He's practically ordered me to go.'

'Tin sheep might be valuable,' said Nautilus. 'Is that a blue monkey you've got there?'

The hairy man sniffed and looked away.

'Any volunteers for the trip?' asked Bason sadly.

Early next morning Bason and his friends launched their boat and sailed away from Tropnecia. They filled it to the gunwales with wine, honey, cakes and water jars,* and the hairy blue man sat up on the figurehead, staring down on the wine-dark sea.

The boat was called the *Hugo*, because it had been built by Hugo the boat-builder, so the adventurers were called the *Hugonauts*. The *Hugo* leaked a bit at the seams, and it was all Bason could do to stop the boat-builder drilling holes in the bottom of his boat to let the water run away.

All that day and the next they sailed westward.

'We've got to go through the Straits of Gibraltar and turn right,' said Bason. 'But now let's stop for the night on that island over there. I'm hungry.'

It was just a large, flat rock, but the Hugonauts

---

* Making sure also to pack slices of quince and a runcible spoon, of course.

tied their boat to it and rushed ashore. Soon they had a fire going, and were passing the wine around.

But Bason felt a bit uneasy about the island, especially when the little blue man padded up to him and pointed to the water. The island was sinking! Just then a great paddle-shaped leg, bigger than the *Hugo*, heaved itself out of the water and splashed down again.

'Back to the boat!' shouted Bason. **'This rock's alive!'**

Before he could say much more the island sank under the waves, putting out the fire, and leaving all the Hugonauts struggling in the water. They scrambled aboard their boat as fast as they could.

And then the *Hugo* started to move through the water.

It's still tied to the island! thought Bason.

'It's called a leviathan,' Nautilus the inventor

was telling the crew.* 'They're giant turtles that go to sleep on the surface, and sometimes people built whole towns on them before they woke up … **Hey!**'

By now the *Hugo* was hardly touching the surface of the water, and Bason was hunting frantically for a knife to cut the mooring rope. But the little blue man rushed past him, jumped into the bows, and sank his teeth into the creaking rope.

There was a **spang!** then a **splash!**, and the *Hugo* was drifting free. But a dark shape rose out of the water some way off, and against the bright stars the Hugonauts saw a great turtle's head, watching them, before it sank out of sight.

As the giant turtle paddled off into the night there was a bubbling noise by the *Hugo*'s bows, and a different head rose out of the water. It was large

---

* It would have been more useful, of course, if he had told them this *before* the turtle decided to swim off. Before their dinner had been cooked too.

and bearded – though the beard and the flowing hair were dark green – and it wore a golden crown studded with pearls.

'What do you mean by invading my kingdom?' it thundered in a voice like a thousand waterfalls.

'I'm sorry,' said Bason, leaning over the side of the boat. 'Sir,' he added.

The King of the Sea frowned. 'What are you doing this far west?' he asked. 'After my fish and pearls, I expect.'

'Oh no, we are going to find the Tin Fleece,' said Bason. 'Out beyond this sea there is an island where there's tin and sheep—'

'I know,' said the king impatiently. 'In that case, the sooner you are gone the better. Hand me that rope.'

All night long the King of the Sea towed the *Hugo* through the water, while Bason and the rest of the crew huddled at the bottom of the boat.

Finally, just as the sun was rising, the king let go of the rope and called for Bason.

'This is the Great Ocean,' he said. 'Sail north, and in a week or two you'll reach the island you want. Take care. If you're in danger, stick your head underwater and call for me.'

'Thank you,' said Bason. 'But why are you helping us?'

'Because when you sail back from the island I shall demand a gift before I let you go back to Tropnecia,' said the King of the Sea. 'And now, to help you on your way, you'll need a good south wind. Whistle.'

Bason did so, feeling a bit of a fool, and above the mast of the *Hugo* a winged figure appeared. He seemed almost transparent because Bason saw a bit of cloud through his chest, and his cheeks were full of wind.

'This is my cousin, Aeolus, the South Wind,' said the king, and with a final 'Farewell!' he sank under the waves.

Aeolus flapped his wings and began to blow.

The *Hugo*'s sail **billowed**, and with the South Wind behind it the boat began to go north.

'I don't like this messing about with winds and kings,' said Nautilus. 'This big wind will want a gift too, and Plous wants the Tin Fleece, and I expect everyone else wants it as well. If we get home with enough money to buy a new shirt I'd be very surprised.'

On and on went the *Hugo*, with the big sad Aeolus flapping behind it. Then one grey day they sighted land.

Then the wind left them, and they had to row, and finally they beached their boat on a rocky shore, where the waves crashed over the pebbles. The sun went behind a cloud and it started to rain. Far away, drums began to beat.

The Hugonauts dragged their boat up the beach and hid it in a cave. The rain **drummed** on the sand. It was not the sort of day to begin exploring.

Nautilus and some of the others went hunting and came back with two scrawny sheep.

'There's an orchard up on the cliff,' said Nautilus, taking handfuls of small red apples from his pockets. 'These are much nicer than the ones we grow at home.'

'They're Grabley's Sunset Wonders,' said the little blue man. Everyone turned and stared.

The small blue hairy man had come with them all the way from Tropnecia, but no one had heard him speak before. Some of the Hugonauts still thought he was an odd kind of monkey.

'They're cider apples,' said the little blue man. 'It's no good eating them. The sheep will be all right with mint sauce. And some nice taties.'

'Do you mean you could talk all the time?' asked Bason.

'Heh heh! The Tin Fleece, eh?' said the little man. 'If you take it you're welcome to it! Take it and welcome!'

That's why he had paddled his coracle to Tropnecia, he told them. The Tin Fleece had caused nothing but trouble since it was made.

'My name is Grimberry,' he said. 'I live just along the coast a bit. This island – Gross Britannica, we call it – is quite big, but there are a lot of kings on it. King Melider had the Tin Fleece made from the metal out of his mines. It hangs on a crab apple tree a long way from here, and it's guarded by a wild cat with copper claws. But that doesn't stop all our young men going and getting themselves killed, trying to get the fleece. King Melider takes all their swords and money.'

'Does it really look like a fleece?' asked Bason.

'Yes, and although it's made out of tin it's as soft as wool,' said Grimberry. 'All the other kings come to take it as well, and trample down our crops.'

'Well, if we can only go back empty-handed we'd much better not go back at all,' said Bason. 'Where is the fleece?'

'First you have to see Melider. But before he lets you see the fleece he sets all kinds of impossible tasks for you to do,' said Grimberry sadly. 'Not many people survive them.'

'Oh dear,' said Bason. 'I suppose you'd better take us to him, then.'

He took Nautilus and Hugo with him, and after

a long trek across fields of brambles they came to the palace of King Melider.

The gates of King Melider's palace swung open as Bason and his friends approached. The king himself stood there, surrounded by his soldiers.

Since Melider owned the Tin Fleece, all his clothes were made of wool. Even his beard and hair looked woolly.

'Good day,' he said to Bason. 'Where are you from?'

'Tropnecia,' said Bason.

'Never heard of it,' said the king, and **YAWNED**. 'Ho-hum. I suppose you're after the fleece? I'll show you where it is if you do a little job for me. I've got a couple of baa-lambs that want shearing. Do that, and I'll take you to the fleece.'

He led Bason and the others to a small field in the palace grounds. There they saw two giant rams, breathing fire and butting each other.

King Melider handed Bason a pair of scissors. 'Don't hurt them,' he said, and hurried away laughing.

'I said he was like that,' said Grimberry.

'Those sheep look like elephants,' said Nautilus.

But Bason **scrambled** over the fence with the scissors held in his teeth.

The moment the rams saw him, they blew out **huge** clouds of flame and charged. And what was worse, one charged from one side, and one the other. It looked as though Bason was going to be squeezed – but at the last moment he took a deep breath and jumped.

The rams met with a clang that broke windows and shook apples off trees a mile away. Birds flew away squawking and the rams staggered back, blinked, and fell over.

Grimberry jumped over the fence and helped Bason tie the rams up before they came round. Then, dodging the horns and the flames, Bason sheared the rams and piled the wool in the middle of the field.

When King Melider saw it he went as white as the wool.

'Now, remember – you must let me see the fleece,' said Bason.

'He's probably got a lot of nasty tricks up his sleeve,' whispered Grimberry. 'Don't trust him an inch!'

King Melider led Bason and his companions to the secret orchard where the Tin Fleece was hidden.

They left the palace and walked up a winding, overgrown path to the cliff tops and came, after a steep climb over bramble-covered rocks, to a cluster of twisted trees. They were bent by the sea wind and each one was covered with small golden apples.

Bason tapped one of the apples with his finger, and it rang. 'I think these are gold,' he said. 'Real gold.'

King Melider said nothing, but **stomped** on.

Suddenly they saw the Tin Fleece. It was spread over the lower boughs of an old bent apple tree, and every tin curl glittered in the bright sunlight.

'It is softer than cloth and warmer than wool,' said King Melider. 'If you can take it from the tree you can keep it.'

So Bason drew his sword and stepped forward. But he had hardly moved before there was a terrible **screech**, and something leaped from the tree.

'It's the wild cat with copper claws!' yelled Grimberry.

Bason jumped away as the cat came at him spitting and scratching, and tried to snatch the fleece. Then through the trees he saw the helmets of Melider's soldiers.

'He's tricked us!' he cried. **'Here come**

his soldiers! Jump for your lives!'

Nautilus peered over the edge of the cliff. 'What about you?'

But just then Bason killed the cat and came running to the cliff edge with the Tin Fleece in his arms. Melider was nowhere to be seen.

Hugo, Nautilus and Grimberry dived into the sea. A moment later, with the Tin Fleece held tightly in one hand, Bason jumped after them.

Bason swam out to the boat just as his friends were clambering aboard, dragging a half-drowned Hugo with them.

'He sank like a stone,' said Grimberry. 'He must weigh a ton!'

Bason threw the Tin Fleece aboard and hauled himself after it. Already he could see King Melider's men hurrying down to the shore where – he saw with a sinking feeling – there were half a dozen sleek blue ships, each with a pair of gilded horns on its prow.

'Row!' he cried, as the Hugonauts unshipped their oars. **'They're after us!'**

The *Hugo* skimmed over the waves with its crew leaning on the oars for all they were worth. But its builder lay at the bottom of the boat, blowing a little fountain, while Bason tried a bit of artificial respiration.

'No wonder he sank,' he said. 'He's been scrumping!'

Large golden apples were rolling out of Hugo's pockets.

'These are from Melider's magic orchard,' said Bason. 'I thought Hugo looked interested in them. Solid gold, by the weight of them.'

Already the enemy fleet was dropping behind,

and the Hugonauts rowed south with light hearts.

'Well, here it is, lads!' said Bason, holding up the Tin Fleece. It sparkled in the sun, and jingled as the wind caught it.

There was a sudden roaring sound and the sea rushed and bubbled. The boat rose out of the water with a jerk, and a great wet head looked over the stern.

'Mine, I think,' said the King of the Sea, pointing to the fleece with a scaly finger. 'Unless, of course, you'd prefer to be eaten by sharks and swordfish.'

A sudden wind sprang up. It was Aeolus, the South Wind, hovering above the boat with outspread wings.

'You promisssed,' he hissed. *'The fleesse is oursss, unless youuu would prefffffer tooo beee blown back toooo yourrr enemiessss!'*

'Now, I'm sure we can come to a sensible arrangement about this,' said Bason, trying to keep his balance as the King of the Sea shook the boat from side to side. 'We'll all be put to death if we return without the fleece.' A sudden idea struck him. 'How about some golden apples? Real gold?'

'Show ussss!'

Bason held out the apples Hugo had taken from Melider's orchard. The King of the Sea and the South Wind looked at them for a long time.

Then the king snatched the apples, tossed the *Hugo* back into the sea, and sank out of sight. The wind died down.

All through the night the Hugonauts rowed south to Tropnecia, leaving King Melider's fleet far behind. It was a dark night with no stars, but Bason could see the dim outline of land in the east. Clouds covered the moon.

'What will King Plous do with the Tin Fleece when we get back?' asked Grimberry.

'Lock it up in one of his underground treasure chambers, I expect,' said Nautilus.

Bason had nailed the fleece to the mast, where it tinkled in the night breeze and reflected stray beams of moonlight.

'It seems a shame,' said Grimberry after a while. 'It looks so nice.'

'If we don't take the Tin Fleece back, the king won't let Bason marry the Princess Eriden,' said Nautilus.

But when the *Hugo* sailed into Tropnecia harbour Bason found that the king had no intention of letting him marry the princess. Instead, he was waiting with a lot of soldiers on the quay.

'Here's the fleece,' said Bason, throwing it

ashore. 'Now will you let me wed Princess Eriden?'

'No,' said the king, but before he could say any more the Hugonauts swarmed ashore, laying about them with their oars and swords, whacking the soldiers into the water. While the battle was going on the harbour lookout ran up.

'There's a lot of blue ships coming!' he cried.

'King Melider's come for his fleece!' said Bason. All fighting forgotten, they hurried down to their boats, and sailed out to meet King Melider.

In the great sea battle that followed outside the harbour walls, King Melider's ship was sunk – and King Plous was killed by an arrow. So when the Gross Britannica ships limped home Tropnecia was left without a king.

So they elected Bason, and he married the princess, and the Hugonauts nailed the Tin Fleece onto a pole in the city centre where everybody could see it. And Grimberry sailed back to Gross Britannica in his coracle, and became king in place of Melider, and there was great friendship between the two countries from that day on.

Enjoyed the stories in
The Time-travelling Caveman?

Read on for an extract from the first story
in another fantastically funny collection from

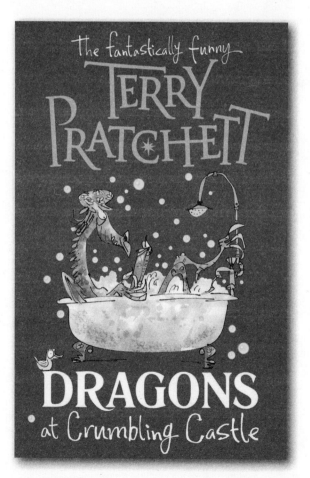

DRAGONS AT CRUMBLING CASTLE

In the days of King Arthur there were no newspapers, only town criers, who went around shouting the news at the tops of their voices.

King Arthur was sitting up in bed one Sunday, eating an egg, when the Sunday town crier trooped in. Actually, there were several of them: a man to draw the pictures, a jester for the jokes and a small man in tights and football boots who was called the Sports Page.

'DRAGONS INVADE CRUMBLING CASTLE,'

shouted the News Crier (this was the headline), and then he said in a softer voice, **'For full details hear page nine.'**

King Arthur dropped his spoon in amazement. **Dragons!** All the knights were out on quests, except for Sir Lancelot – and he had gone to France for his holidays.

The Ninth Page came panting up, coughed, and said: 'Thousands flee for their lives as family of green dragons burn and rampage around Crumbling Castle . . .'

'What is King Arthur doing about this?' demanded the Editorial Crier pompously. 'What do we pay our taxes for? The people of Camelot demand action . . .'

'Throw them out, and give them fourpence* each,' said the king to the butler. 'Then call out the guard.'

Later that day he went out to the courtyard.

'Now then, men,' he said. 'I want a volunteer . . .' Then he adjusted his spectacles. The only other person in the courtyard was a small boy in a suit of mail much too big for him.

'Ralph reporting, sire!' the lad said, and saluted. 'Where's everyone else?'

'Tom, John, Ron, Fred, Bill and Jack are off

---

* In the days of King Arthur, this was a lot more money than it seems today – it would buy, oh, at least a cup of mead and a hunk of goat's meat.

sick,' said Ralph, counting on his fingers. 'Then William, Bert, Joe and Albert are on holiday. James is visiting his granny. Rupert has gone hunting. And Eric . . .'

'Well then,' said the king. 'Ralph, how would you like to visit Crumbling Castle? Nice scenery, excellent food, only a few dragons to kill. Take my spare suit of armour – it's a bit roomy, but quite thick . . .'

So Ralph got on his donkey and trotted over the drawbridge, whistling, and disappeared over the hills. When he was out of sight he took off the armour and hid it behind a hedge, because it squeaked and was too hot, and put on his ordinary clothes.

High on a wooded hill sat a mounted figure in coal-black armour. He watched the young boy pass by, then galloped down after him on his big black horse.

'HALT IN THE NAME OF THE FRIDAY KNIGHT,'

he cried in a deep voice, raising his black sword.

Ralph looked round. 'Excuse me, sir,' he said. 'Is this the right road to Crumbling Castle?'

'Well, yes, actually it is,' said the knight, looking rather embarrassed, and then he remembered that he was really a big bad knight, and continued in a hollow voice,

'BUT YOU'LL HAVE TO FIGHT ME FIRST!'

Ralph looked up in amazement as the black knight got off his horse and charged at him, waving his sword.

'Yield!' the knight yelled, then he got his foot stuck in a rabbit hole and tripped over in a great clatter, like an explosion in a tin factory. Bits of armour flew everywhere.

There was silence for a moment, and then the helmet unscrewed itself and Ralph saw that the Friday knight himself was a very small man indeed. Or, at least, he had a very small head.

'Sorry,' said the knight. 'Can I try again?'

'Certainly not!' said Ralph, and unsheathed his rusty sword. 'I've won. You've fallen over first.* It's not even Friday, so I shall call you Fortnight, 'cos I've fought you tonight. You're my prisoner!'

There was a great deal of clanking inside the armour, and then Fortnight climbed out through a trap door in the back. His ferocious black armour was three times as big as he was.

* That's how it went in those days: the first knight to fall over lost the fight. I bet you all knew that.

So Ralph continued his journey to Crumbling Castle on his donkey, followed by Fortnight the Friday knight on his great black charger. After a while they became quite friendly, because Fortnight knew lots of jokes and could sing quite well. He'd belonged to a circus before he became a knight.

Next day they found a wizard sitting on a milestone, reading a book. He had the normal wizard's uniform: long white beard, pointed hat,* a sort of nightdress covered in signs and spells, and long floppy boots, which he had taken off, revealing red socks.

'Excuse me, sir,' said Ralph, because you have to be careful when talking to wizards. 'Is this the way to Crumbling Castle?'

---

* No self-respecting wizard would be seen in public without a pointy hat. But it could make going through low doorways a bit tricky, so they often developed bad knees in later life due to all that crouching down.

Look out for more short-story collections from the wonderful

TERRY PRATCHETT

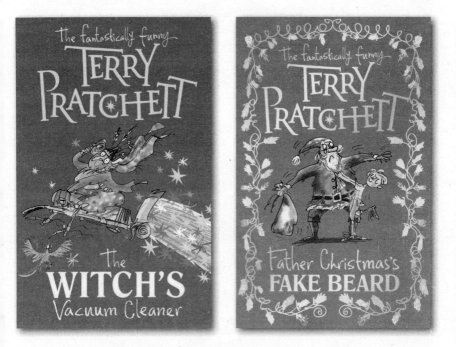

From **magic** and **mayhem**, to **chaos** at **Christmas!**